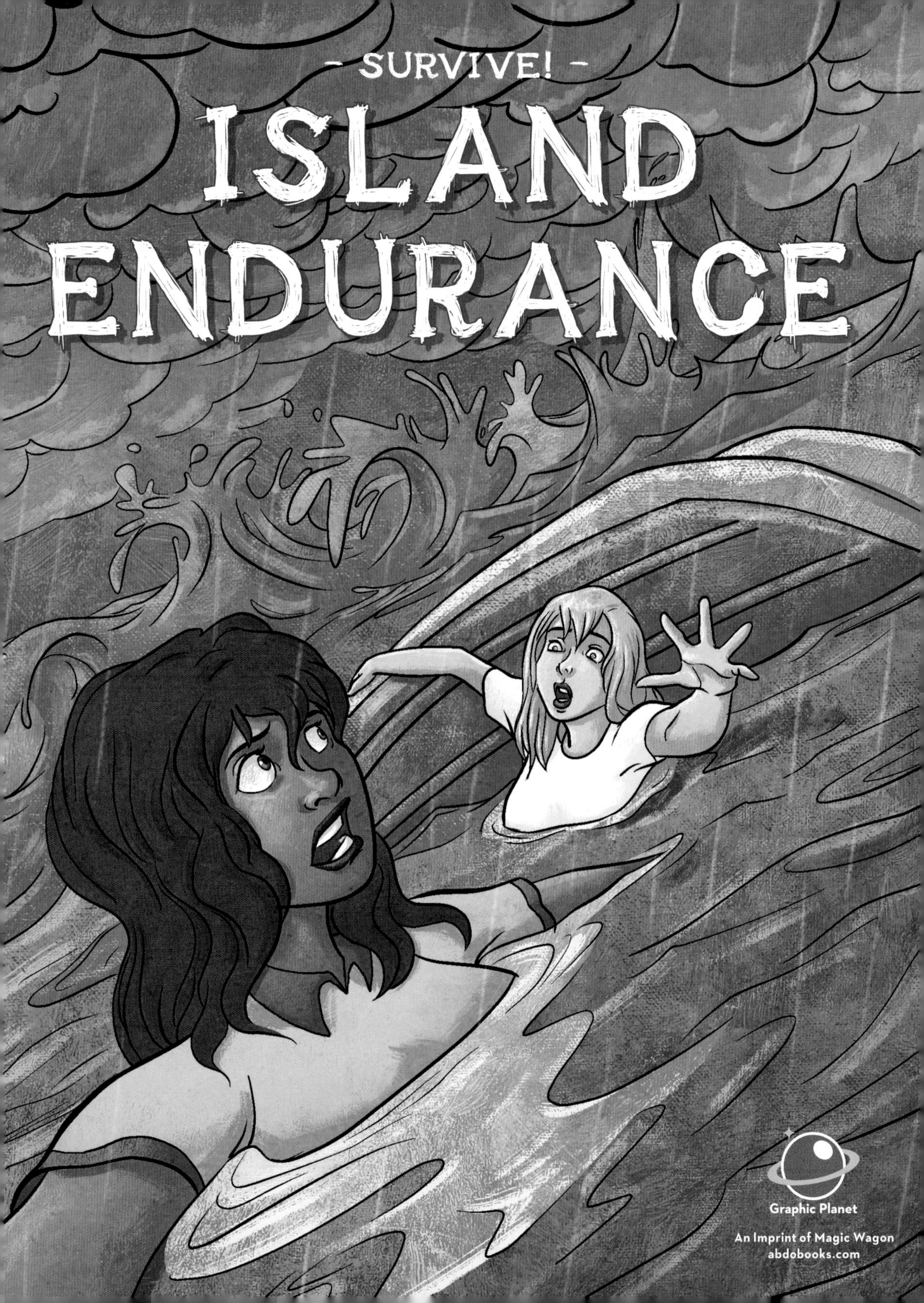
- SURVIVE! -
ISLAND ENDURANCE
Graphic Planet
An Imprint of Magic Wagon
abdobooks.com

abdobooks.com

Published by Magic Wagon, a division of ABDO, PO Box 398166, Minneapolis, Minnesota 55439.
Copyright © 2020 by Abdo Consulting Group, Inc. International copyrights reserved in all countries.
No part of this book may be reproduced in any form without written permission from the publisher.
Graphic Planet™ is a trademark and logo of Magic Wagon.

Printed in the United States of America, North Mankato, Minnesota.
052019
092019

Written by Bill Yu
Illustrated by Thiago Vale and Yonami, with Grafimated
Colored by Dal Bello
Lettered by Kathryn S. Renta
Editorial supervision by David Campiti
Packaged by Glass House Graphics
Art Directed by Christina Doffing
Editorial Support by Tamara L. Britton

Library of Congress Control Number: 2018965023

Publisher's Cataloging-in-Publication Data
Names: Yu, Bill, author. |Bello, Dal; Vale illustrator.
Title: Island endurance / by Bill Yu; illustrated by Dal Bello and Vale.
Description: Minneapolis, Minnesota : Magic Wagon, 2020. | Series: Survive!
Summary: Valerie's father owns a famous resort in the Florida Keys. Merissa works at the resort to fund
    her education. Valerie is a bit self-centered and does not treat the resort's employees with much
    respect. Then an unexpected storm strands Valerie and Merissa on a deserted island. Can they
    survive?
Identifiers: ISBN 9781532135132 (lib. bdg.) | ISBN 9781644941416 (pbk.) | ISBN
    9781532135736 (ebook) | ISBN 9781532136030 (Read-to-Me ebook)
Subjects: LCSH: Resorts--Juvenile fiction. | Florida Keys (Fla.)--Juvenile fiction. | Discourteous
    behavior--Juvenile fiction. | Shipwreck survival--Juvenile fiction. | Survival skills--Juvenile fiction.
Classification: DDC 741.5--dc23

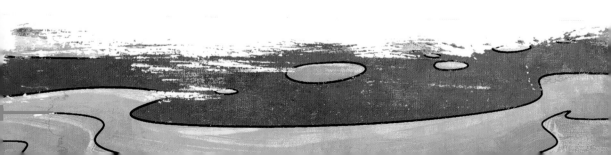

TABLE OF CONTENTS

True Tales of
Survival

You never know when you'll need outdoor survival skills. Sometimes you'll be prepared, other times you won't!

When Being Right Goes Wrong...

Alexander Selkirk was a sailor on Captain Thomas Stradling's ship in the early 1700s. As they explored, the captain stopped for more supplies. Selkirk was concerned that they had too much weight on the ship. He convinced the captain he was right, and Captain Stradling got rid of the extra weight... by stranding Selkirk on the Island of Juan Fernandez! Fortunately, Selkirk was a skilled sailor and was able to survive by making huts out of pimento trees and eating seafood. Later, he found goats which provided clothing, milk, and meat. Four years later on February 1, 1709, he was rescued. He became famous for his story of survival, and inspired the novels *Robinson Crusoe* and *Gulliver's Travels*!

Swiss Family Robinson?
No, Scottish Family Robertson!

In 1971, the Robertson family set sail on their yacht *Lucette* on a voyage around the world. A year and half into their amazing journey, a pod of orca whales sank their boat near the Galápagos Islands. The family escaped on a little raft and a dinghy. They only had 10 days' worth of water and some fruits, candies, and biscuits. When that ran out, they survived on rainwater, turtles, and flying fish. Fortunately,

the dad of the family, Douglas Robertson, was an experienced sailor. The children's mother, Lyn, was a nurse. Together, they ensured that everyone survived. Thirty-eight days later, Japanese fishers spotted the family and they all lived to tell a tale of a family misadventure!

Inuit Can Do It!

In 1921, Inuit woman Ada Blackjack took a job as a cook and seamstress for a team of explorers. She needed money to get treatment for her son, who had tuberculosis. The explorers set off in search of Wrangel Island. They wanted to claim the island for Canada. Unfortunately, they weren't well prepared. They ran out of food, and were unsuccessful at hunting. On an island in Siberia, the team left Ada with a sick explorer and went for help. The explorer didn't survive. But Ada trapped small animals for food. She became skilled at using a gun to hunt birds and seals, and also fight off polar bears! Two years later, her team sent a man to rescue her. She survived, and had earned enough money for her son to be treated in a Seattle hospital!

ISLAND ENDURANCE

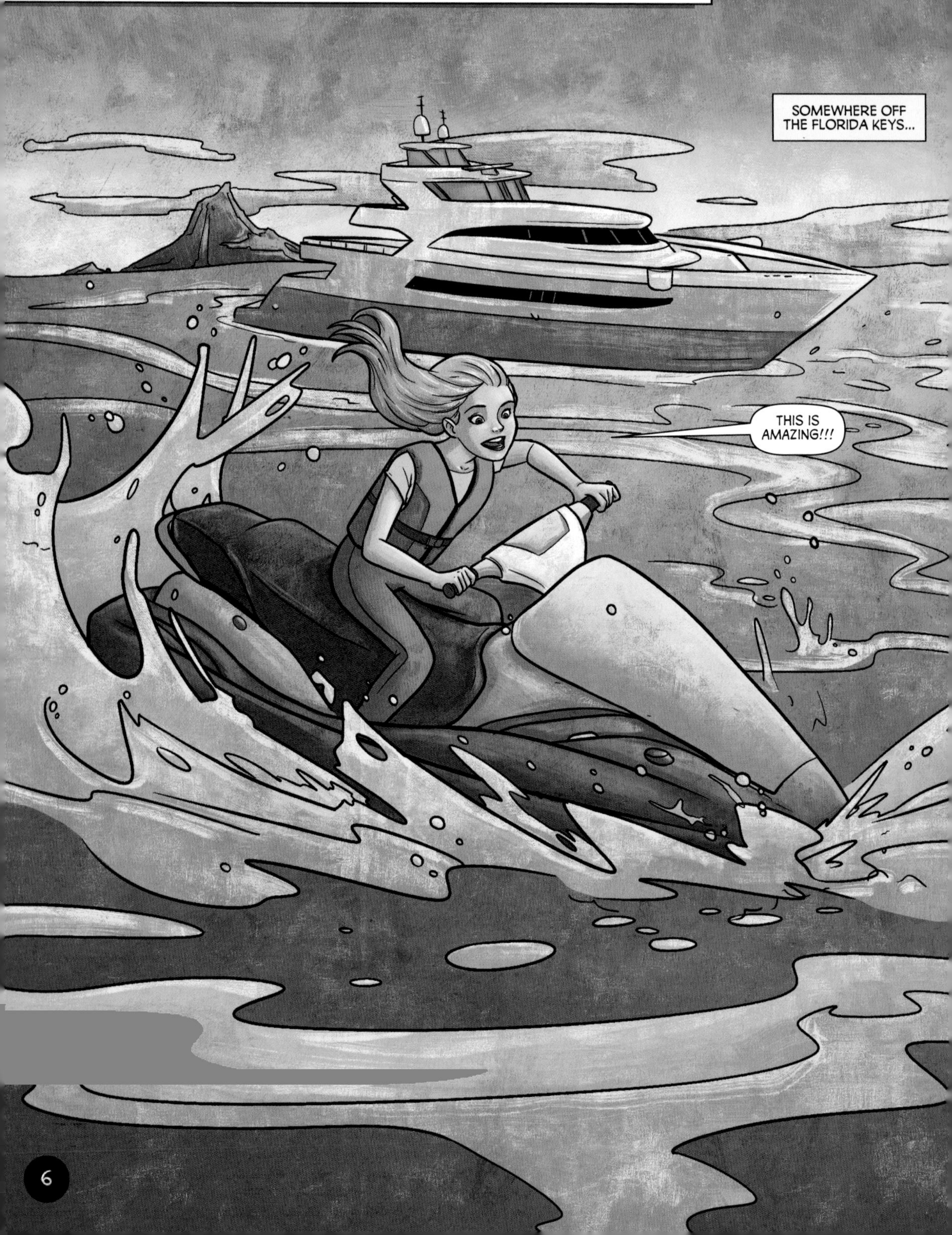
SOMEWHERE OFF THE FLORIDA KEYS...
THIS IS AMAZING!!!

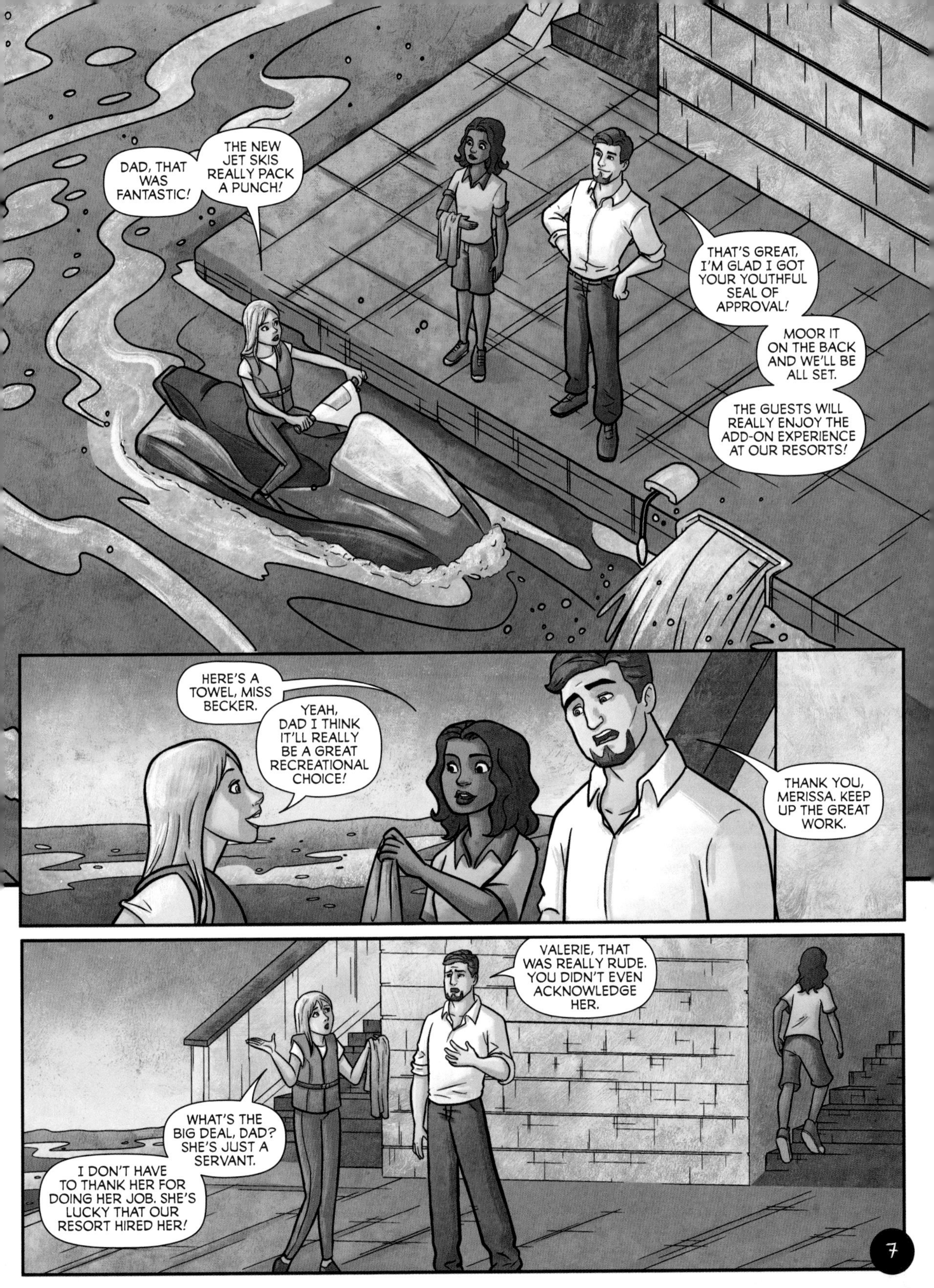
DAD, THAT WAS FANTASTIC!
THE NEW JET SKIS REALLY PACK A PUNCH!
THAT'S GREAT, I'M GLAD I GOT YOUR YOUTHFUL SEAL OF APPROVAL!
MOOR IT ON THE BACK AND WE'LL BE ALL SET.
THE GUESTS WILL REALLY ENJOY THE ADD-ON EXPERIENCE AT OUR RESORTS!
HERE'S A TOWEL, MISS BECKER.
YEAH, DAD I THINK IT'LL REALLY BE A GREAT RECREATIONAL CHOICE!
THANK YOU, MERISSA. KEEP UP THE GREAT WORK.
VALERIE, THAT WAS REALLY RUDE. YOU DIDN'T EVEN ACKNOWLEDGE HER.
WHAT'S THE BIG DEAL, DAD? SHE'S JUST A SERVANT.
I DON'T HAVE TO THANK HER FOR DOING HER JOB. SHE'S LUCKY THAT OUR RESORT HIRED HER!

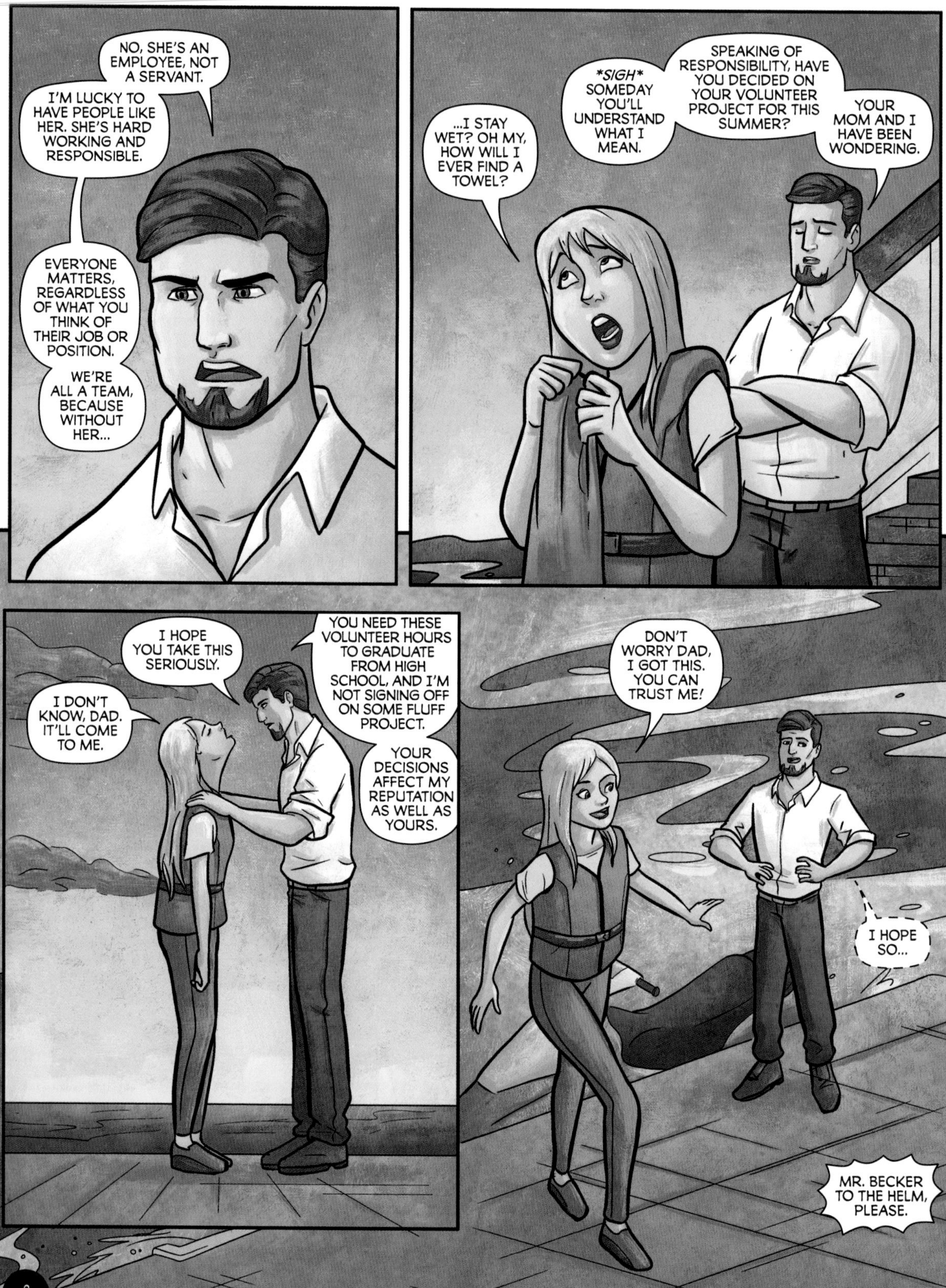
NO, SHE'S AN EMPLOYEE, NOT A SERVANT.
I'M LUCKY TO HAVE PEOPLE LIKE HER. SHE'S HARD WORKING AND RESPONSIBLE.
EVERYONE MATTERS, REGARDLESS OF WHAT YOU THINK OF THEIR JOB OR POSITION.
WE'RE ALL A TEAM, BECAUSE WITHOUT HER...
...I STAY WET? OH MY, HOW WILL I EVER FIND A TOWEL?
SIGH SOMEDAY YOU'LL UNDERSTAND WHAT I MEAN.
SPEAKING OF RESPONSIBILITY, HAVE YOU DECIDED ON YOUR VOLUNTEER PROJECT FOR THIS SUMMER?
YOUR MOM AND I HAVE BEEN WONDERING.
I DON'T KNOW, DAD. IT'LL COME TO ME.
I HOPE YOU TAKE THIS SERIOUSLY.
YOU NEED THESE VOLUNTEER HOURS TO GRADUATE FROM HIGH SCHOOL, AND I'M NOT SIGNING OFF ON SOME FLUFF PROJECT.
YOUR DECISIONS AFFECT MY REPUTATION AS WELL AS YOURS.
DON'T WORRY DAD, I GOT THIS. YOU CAN TRUST ME!
I HOPE SO...
MR. BECKER TO THE HELM, PLEASE.

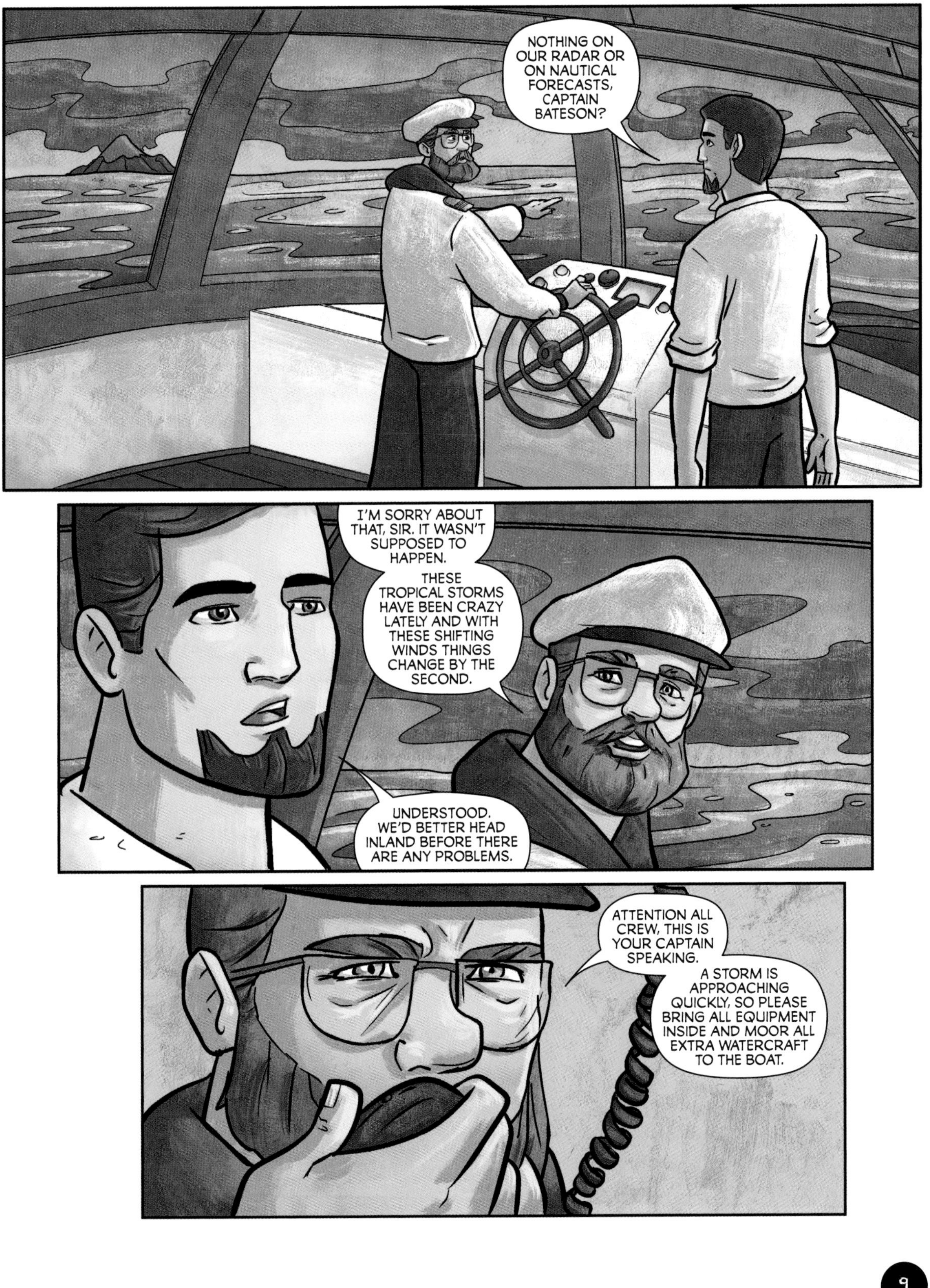
NOTHING ON OUR RADAR OR ON NAUTICAL FORECASTS, CAPTAIN BATESON?
I'M SORRY ABOUT THAT, SIR. IT WASN'T SUPPOSED TO HAPPEN.
THESE TROPICAL STORMS HAVE BEEN CRAZY LATELY AND WITH THESE SHIFTING WINDS THINGS CHANGE BY THE SECOND.
UNDERSTOOD. WE'D BETTER HEAD INLAND BEFORE THERE ARE ANY PROBLEMS.
ATTENTION ALL CREW, THIS IS YOUR CAPTAIN SPEAKING.
A STORM IS APPROACHING QUICKLY, SO PLEASE BRING ALL EQUIPMENT INSIDE AND MOOR ALL EXTRA WATERCRAFT TO THE BOAT.

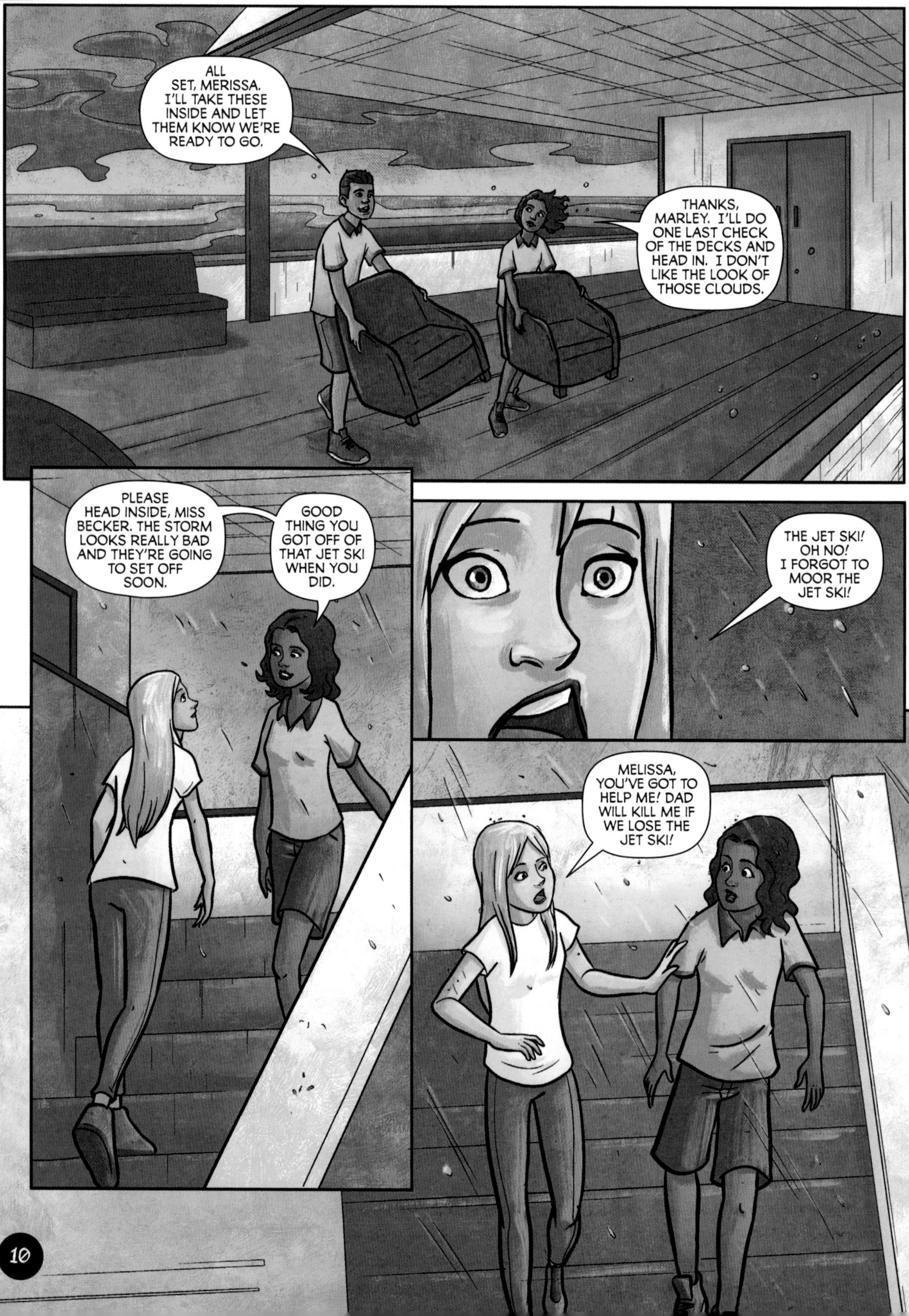
ALL SET, MERISSA. I'LL TAKE THESE INSIDE AND LET THEM KNOW WE'RE READY TO GO.
THANKS, MARLEY. I'LL DO ONE LAST CHECK OF THE DECKS AND HEAD IN. I DON'T LIKE THE LOOK OF THOSE CLOUDS.
PLEASE HEAD INSIDE, MISS BECKER. THE STORM LOOKS REALLY BAD AND THEY'RE GOING TO SET OFF SOON.
GOOD THING YOU GOT OFF OF THAT JET SKI WHEN YOU DID.
THE JET SKI! OH NO! I FORGOT TO MOOR THE JET SKI!
MELISSA, YOU'VE GOT TO HELP ME! DAD WILL KILL ME IF WE LOSE THE JET SKI!

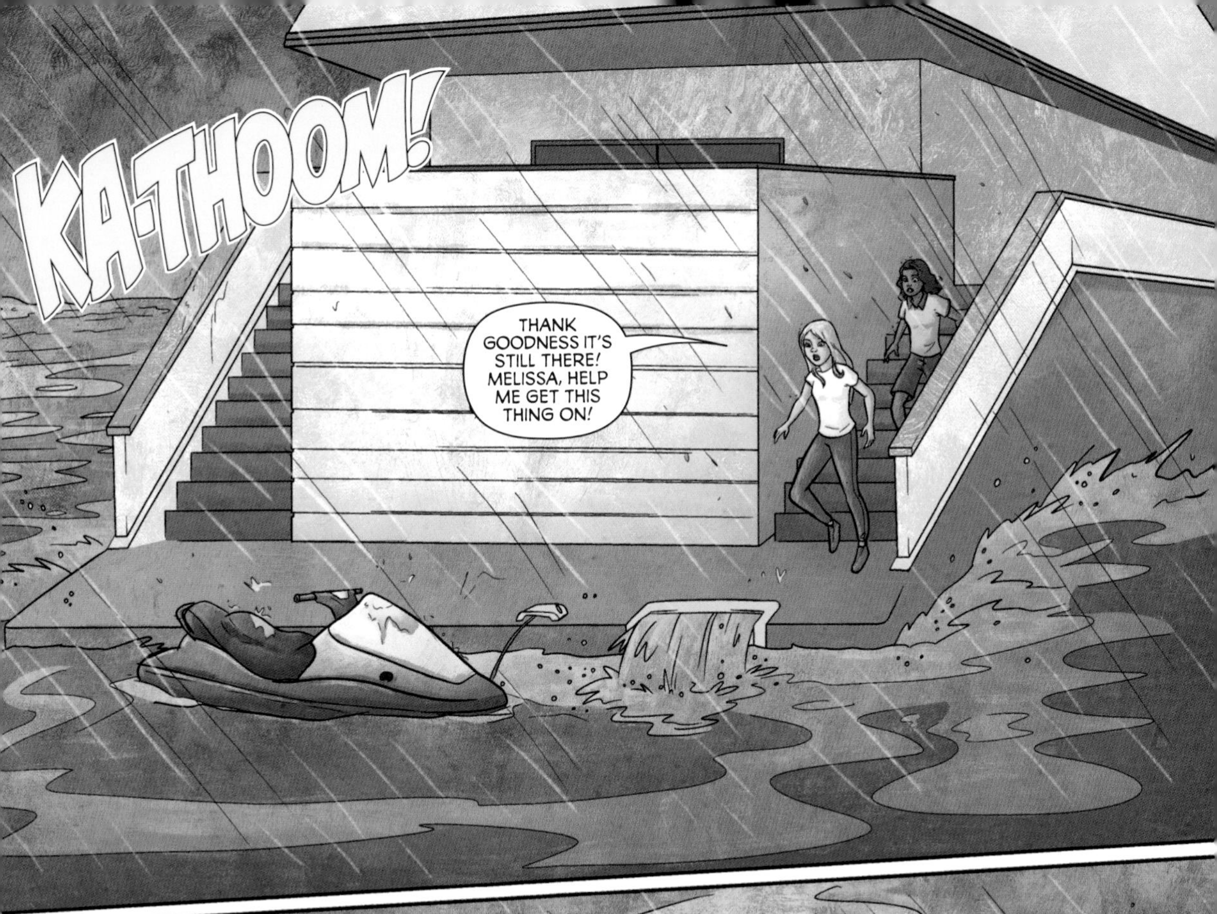
KA-THOOM!
THANK GOODNESS IT'S STILL THERE! MELISSA, HELP ME GET THIS THING ON!

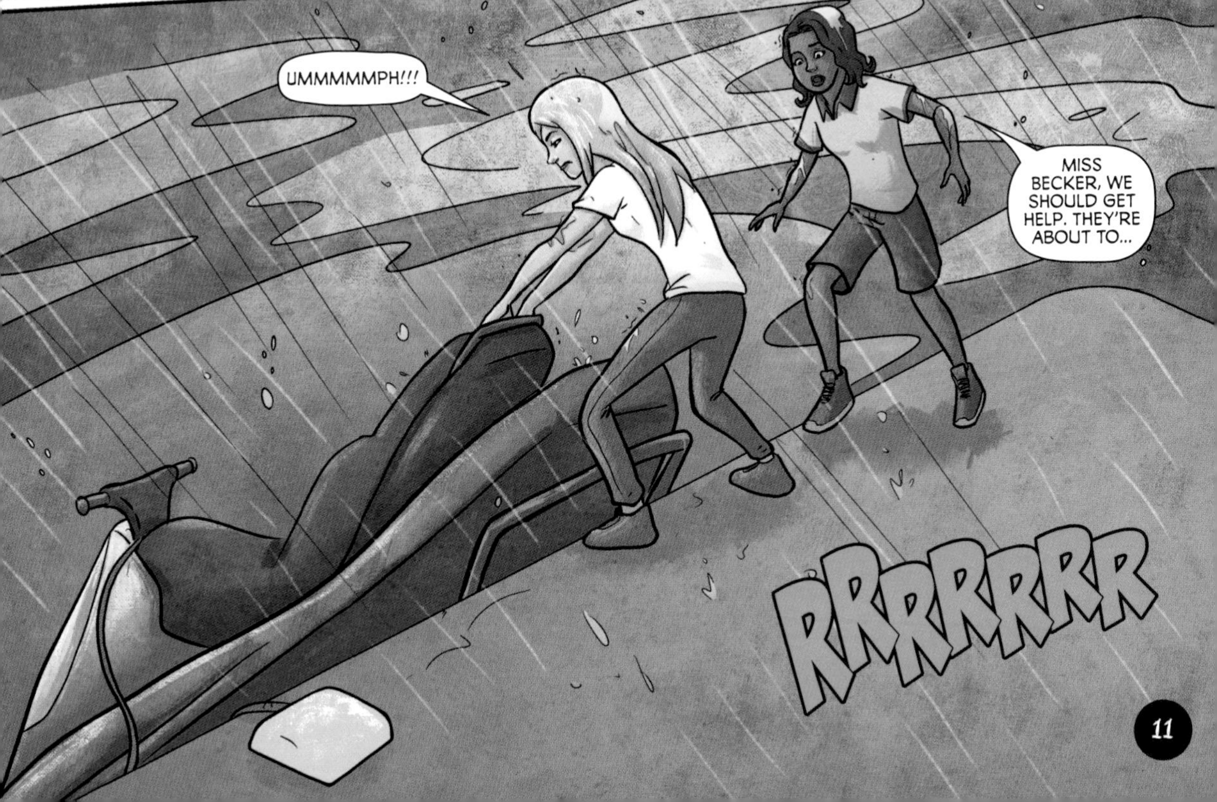
UMMMMMPH!!!
MISS BECKER, WE SHOULD GET HELP. THEY'RE ABOUT TO...
RRRRRRR

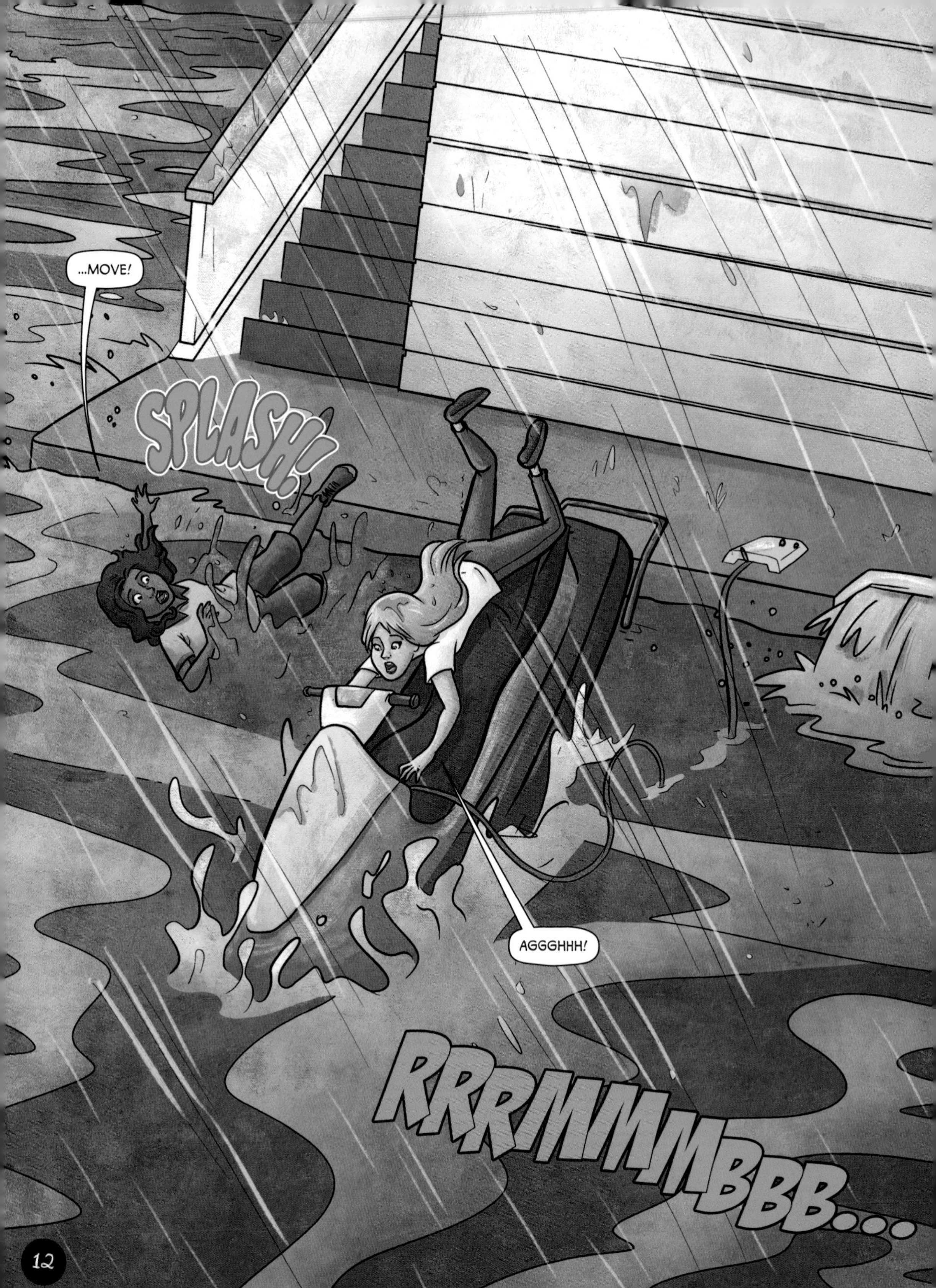
...MOVE!
SPLASH!
AGGGHHH!
RRRMMMMBBB...

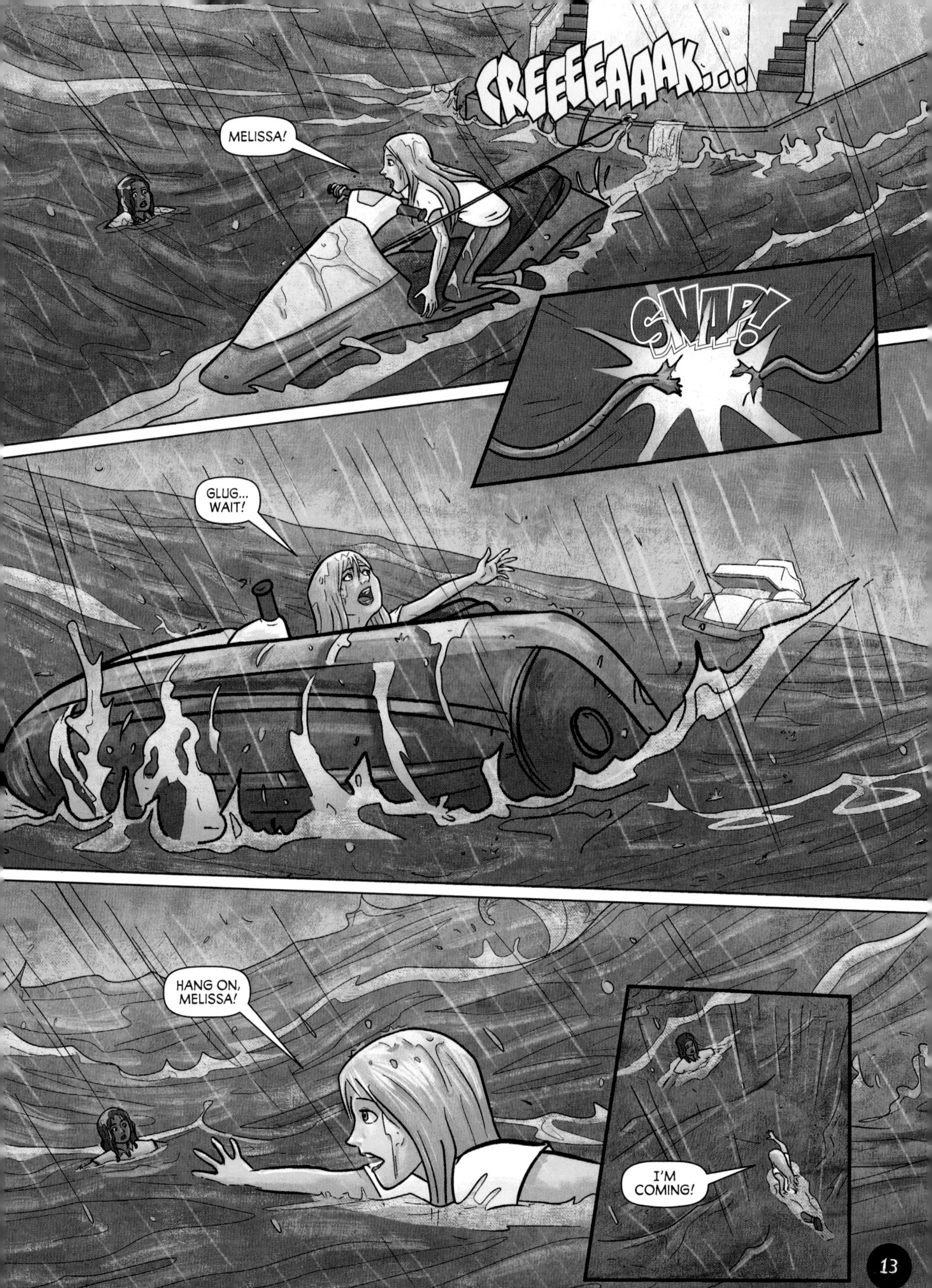
CREEEEAAAK...
MELISSA!
SNAP!
GLUG... WAIT!
HANG ON, MELISSA!
I'M COMING!

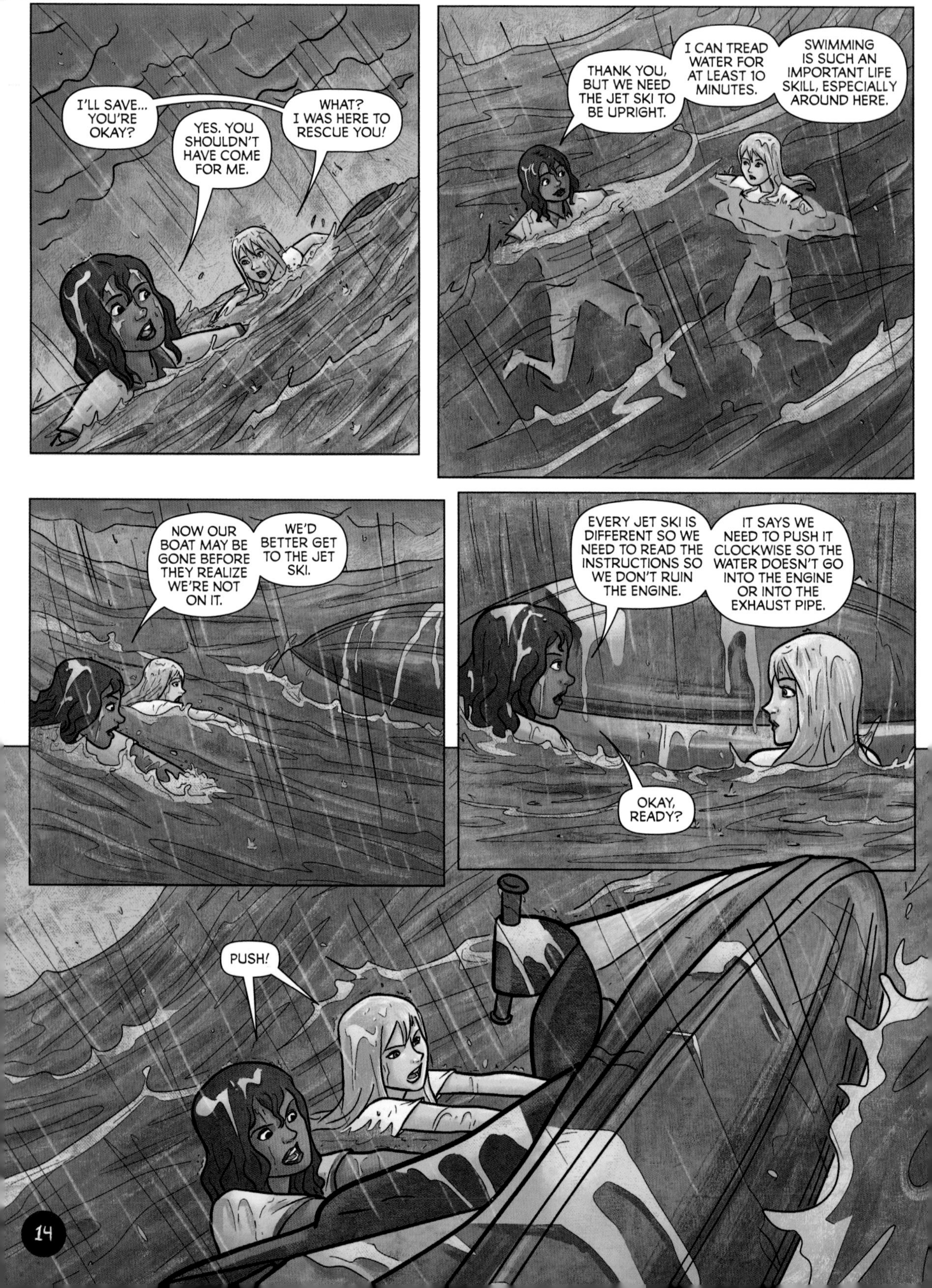
I'LL SAVE... YOU'RE OKAY?
YES. YOU SHOULDN'T HAVE COME FOR ME.
WHAT? I WAS HERE TO RESCUE YOU!
THANK YOU, BUT WE NEED THE JET SKI TO BE UPRIGHT.
I CAN TREAD WATER FOR AT LEAST 10 MINUTES.
SWIMMING IS SUCH AN IMPORTANT LIFE SKILL, ESPECIALLY AROUND HERE.
NOW OUR BOAT MAY BE GONE BEFORE THEY REALIZE WE'RE NOT ON IT.
WE'D BETTER GET TO THE JET SKI.
EVERY JET SKI IS DIFFERENT SO WE NEED TO READ THE INSTRUCTIONS SO WE DON'T RUIN THE ENGINE.
IT SAYS WE NEED TO PUSH IT CLOCKWISE SO THE WATER DOESN'T GO INTO THE ENGINE OR INTO THE EXHAUST PIPE.
OKAY, READY?
PUSH!

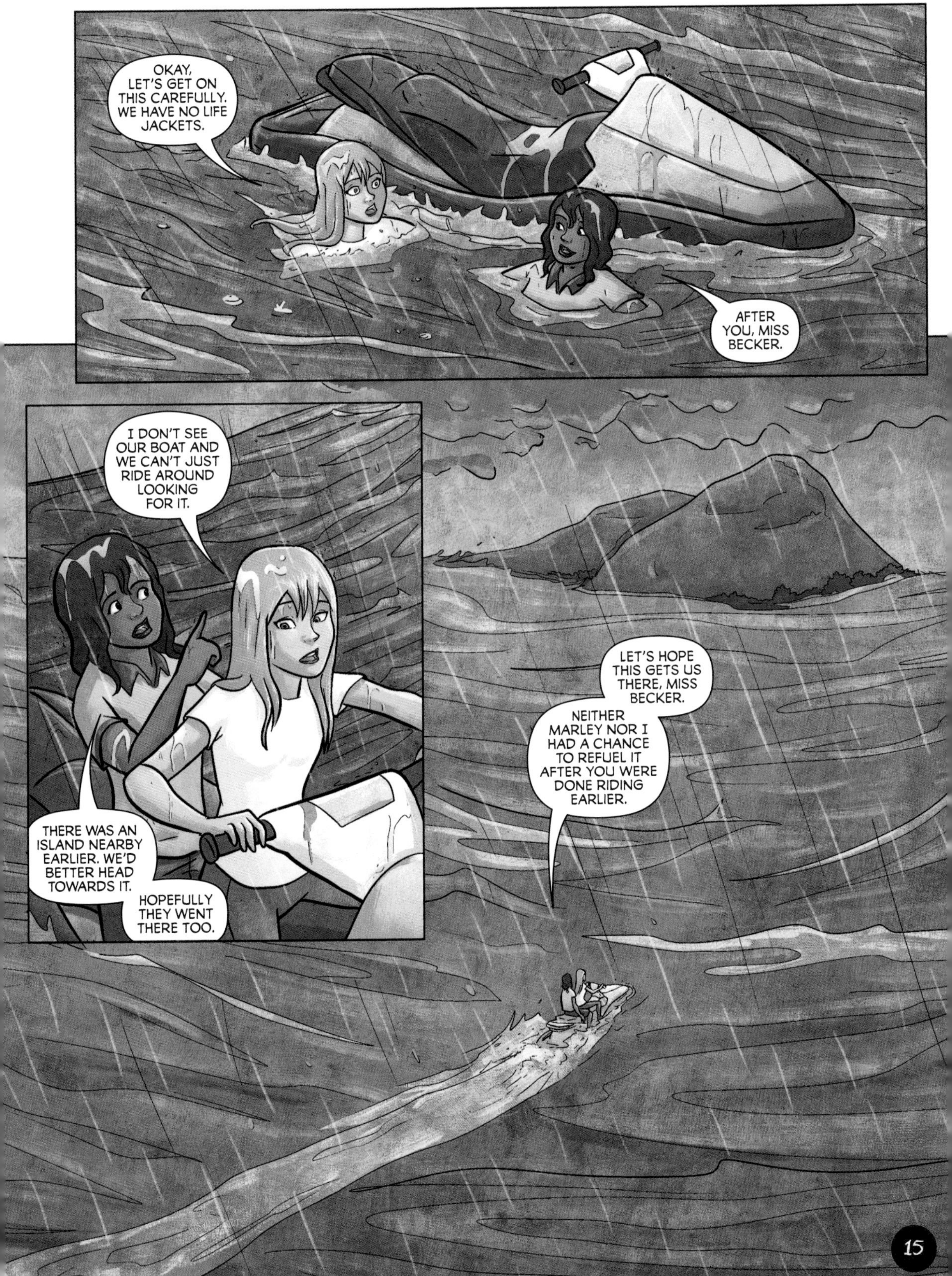
OKAY, LET'S GET ON THIS CAREFULLY. WE HAVE NO LIFE JACKETS.
AFTER YOU, MISS BECKER.
I DON'T SEE OUR BOAT AND WE CAN'T JUST RIDE AROUND LOOKING FOR IT.
THERE WAS AN ISLAND NEARBY EARLIER. WE'D BETTER HEAD TOWARDS IT.
HOPEFULLY THEY WENT THERE TOO.
LET'S HOPE THIS GETS US THERE, MISS BECKER.
NEITHER MARLEY NOR I HAD A CHANCE TO REFUEL IT AFTER YOU WERE DONE RIDING EARLIER.

LATER...
THE GOOD NEWS IS WE MADE IT TO THIS ISLAND. THE BAD NEWS IS THEY'RE NOT HERE.
PLUS WE'RE OUT OF FUEL, MISS BECKER.
MELISSA, WE'RE STRANDED ON A DESERTED ISLAND. YOU CAN CALL ME VALERIE.
YES, MISS... VALERIE. IT'S MERISSA, BY THE WAY.
WHAT?
IT'S MERISSA, NOT MELISSA. MERISSA SEARS.
I'M SORRY, I DIDN'T KNOW.
PERHAPS THERE'S A LOT WE DON'T KNOW ABOUT EACH OTHER... VALERIE.

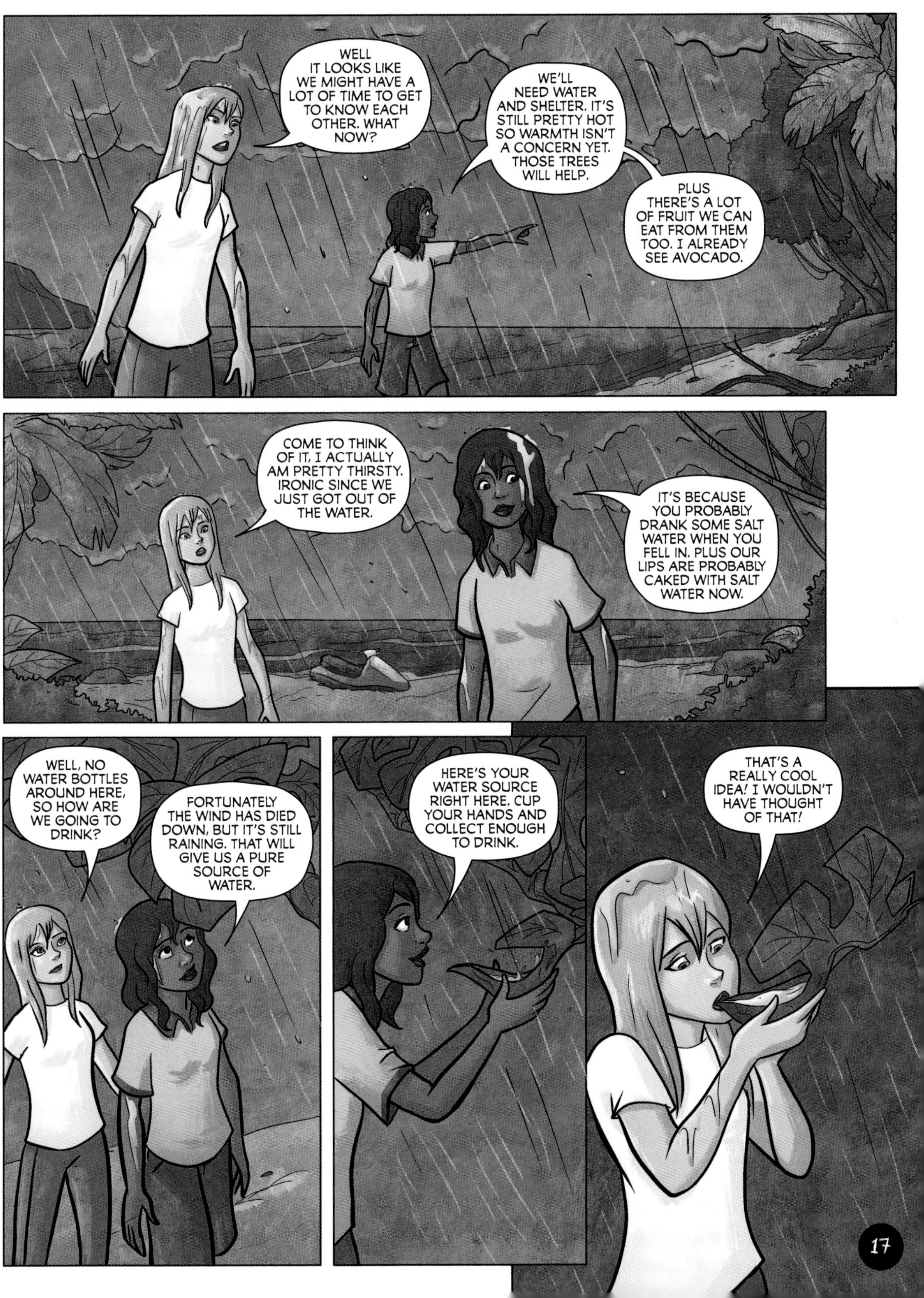
WELL IT LOOKS LIKE WE MIGHT HAVE A LOT OF TIME TO GET TO KNOW EACH OTHER. WHAT NOW?
WE'LL NEED WATER AND SHELTER. IT'S STILL PRETTY HOT SO WARMTH ISN'T A CONCERN YET. THOSE TREES WILL HELP.
PLUS THERE'S A LOT OF FRUIT WE CAN EAT FROM THEM TOO. I ALREADY SEE AVOCADO.
COME TO THINK OF IT, I ACTUALLY AM PRETTY THIRSTY. IRONIC SINCE WE JUST GOT OUT OF THE WATER.
IT'S BECAUSE YOU PROBABLY DRANK SOME SALT WATER WHEN YOU FELL IN. PLUS OUR LIPS ARE PROBABLY CAKED WITH SALT WATER NOW.
WELL, NO WATER BOTTLES AROUND HERE, SO HOW ARE WE GOING TO DRINK?
FORTUNATELY THE WIND HAS DIED DOWN, BUT IT'S STILL RAINING. THAT WILL GIVE US A PURE SOURCE OF WATER.
HERE'S YOUR WATER SOURCE RIGHT HERE. CUP YOUR HANDS AND COLLECT ENOUGH TO DRINK.
THAT'S A REALLY COOL IDEA! I WOULDN'T HAVE THOUGHT OF THAT!

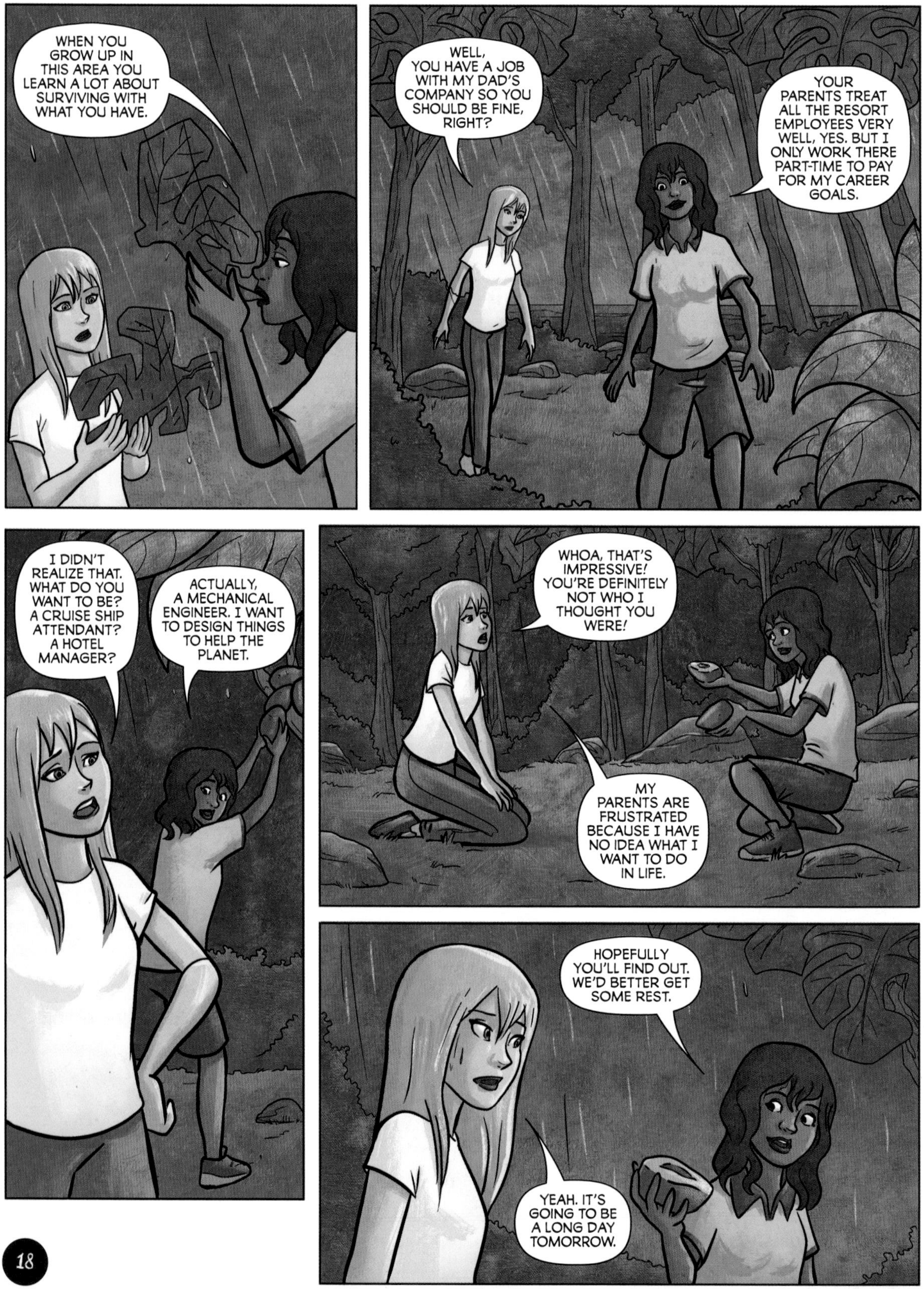
WHEN YOU GROW UP IN THIS AREA YOU LEARN A LOT ABOUT SURVIVING WITH WHAT YOU HAVE.
WELL, YOU HAVE A JOB WITH MY DAD'S COMPANY SO YOU SHOULD BE FINE, RIGHT?
YOUR PARENTS TREAT ALL THE RESORT EMPLOYEES VERY WELL, YES. BUT I ONLY WORK THERE PART-TIME TO PAY FOR MY CAREER GOALS.
I DIDN'T REALIZE THAT. WHAT DO YOU WANT TO BE? A CRUISE SHIP ATTENDANT? A HOTEL MANAGER?
ACTUALLY, A MECHANICAL ENGINEER. I WANT TO DESIGN THINGS TO HELP THE PLANET.
WHOA, THAT'S IMPRESSIVE! YOU'RE DEFINITELY NOT WHO I THOUGHT YOU WERE!
MY PARENTS ARE FRUSTRATED BECAUSE I HAVE NO IDEA WHAT I WANT TO DO IN LIFE.
HOPEFULLY YOU'LL FIND OUT. WE'D BETTER GET SOME REST.
YEAH. IT'S GOING TO BE A LONG DAY TOMORROW.

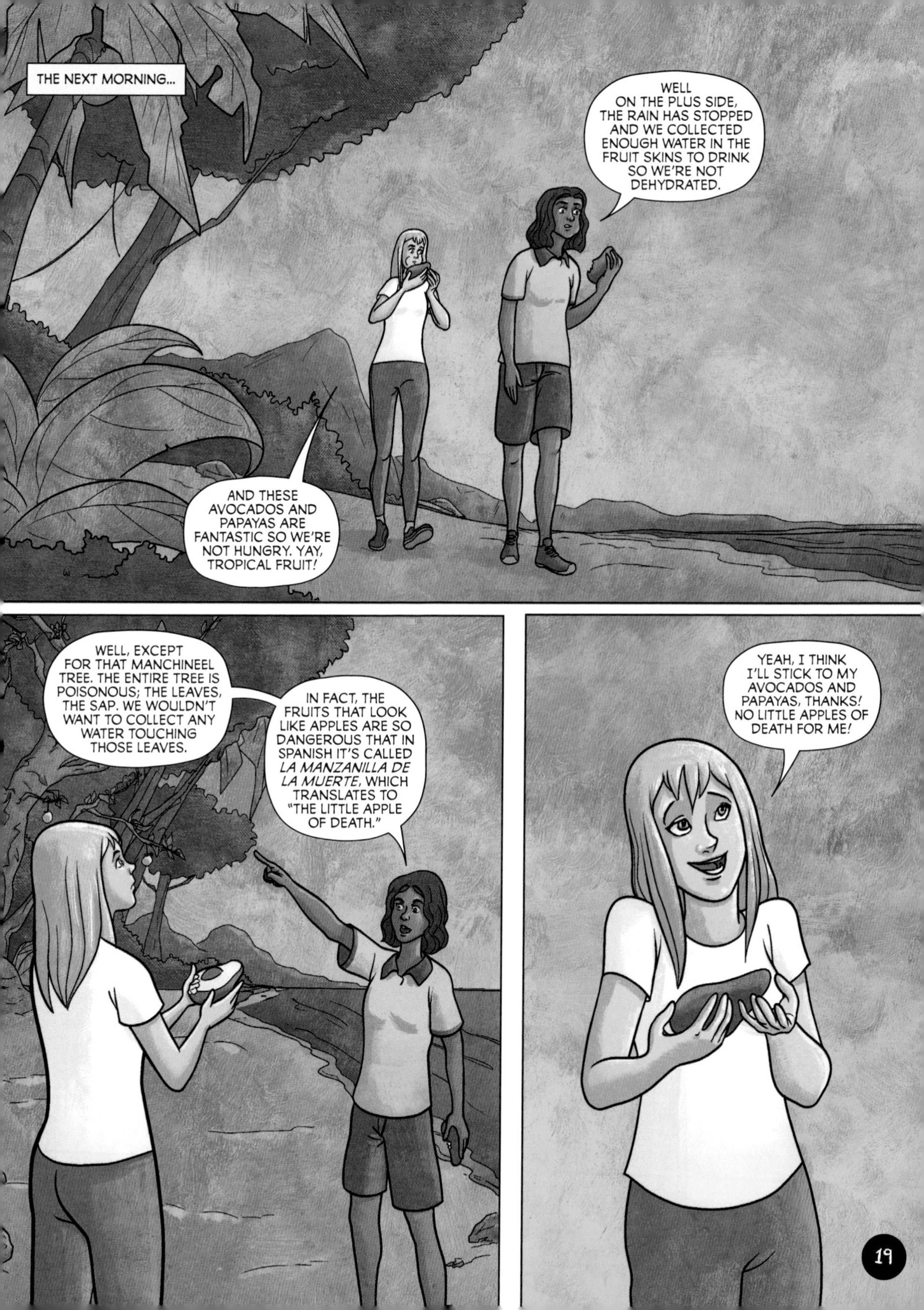
THE NEXT MORNING...
WELL ON THE PLUS SIDE, THE RAIN HAS STOPPED AND WE COLLECTED ENOUGH WATER IN THE FRUIT SKINS TO DRINK SO WE'RE NOT DEHYDRATED.
AND THESE AVOCADOS AND PAPAYAS ARE FANTASTIC SO WE'RE NOT HUNGRY. YAY, TROPICAL FRUIT!
WELL, EXCEPT FOR THAT MANCHINEEL TREE. THE ENTIRE TREE IS POISONOUS; THE LEAVES, THE SAP. WE WOULDN'T WANT TO COLLECT ANY WATER TOUCHING THOSE LEAVES.
IN FACT, THE FRUITS THAT LOOK LIKE APPLES ARE SO DANGEROUS THAT IN SPANISH IT'S CALLED *LA MANZANILLA DE LA MUERTE*, WHICH TRANSLATES TO "THE LITTLE APPLE OF DEATH."
YEAH, I THINK I'LL STICK TO MY AVOCADOS AND PAPAYAS, THANKS! NO LITTLE APPLES OF DEATH FOR ME!

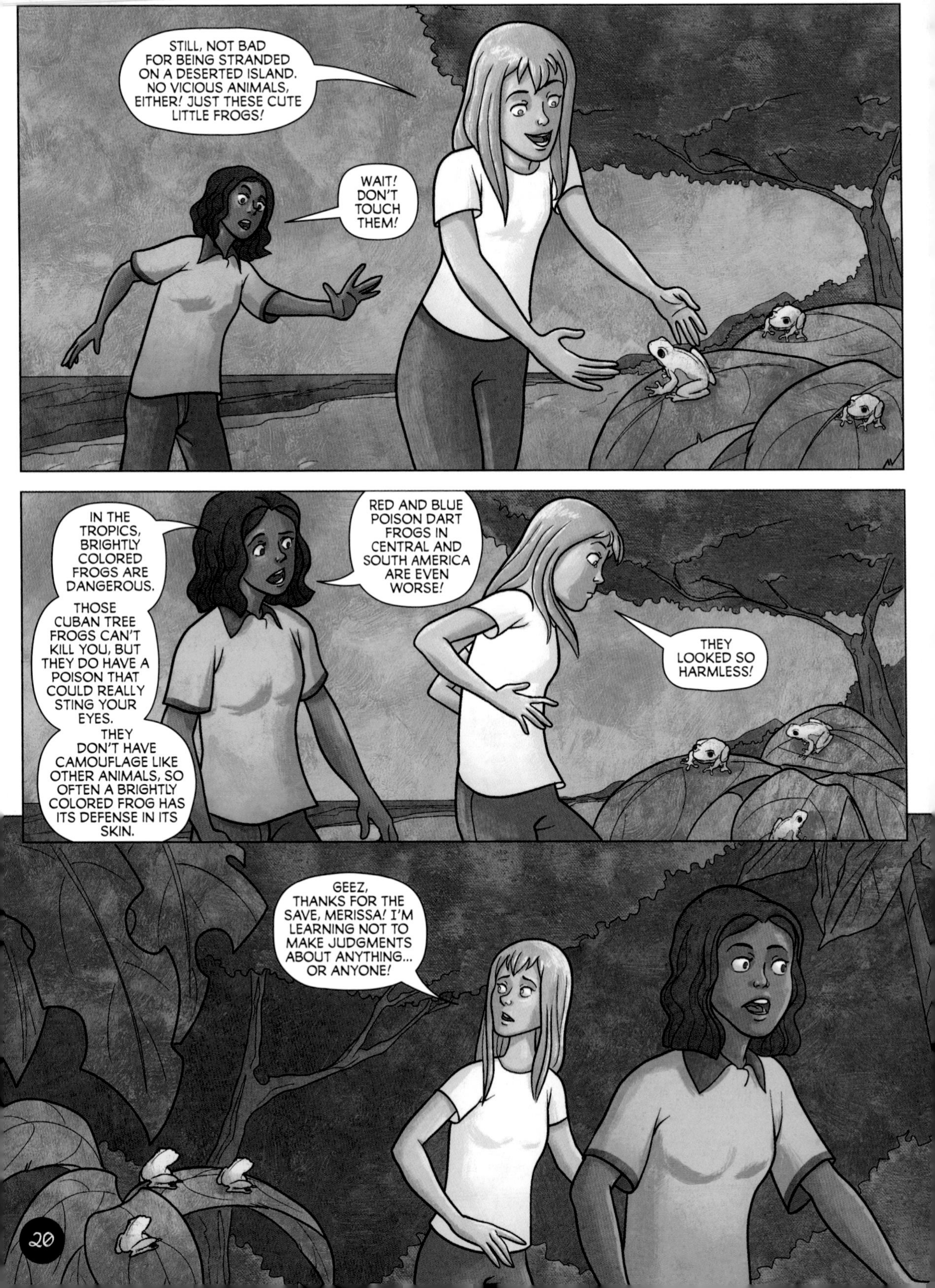
STILL, NOT BAD FOR BEING STRANDED ON A DESERTED ISLAND. NO VICIOUS ANIMALS, EITHER! JUST THESE CUTE LITTLE FROGS!
WAIT! DON'T TOUCH THEM!
IN THE TROPICS, BRIGHTLY COLORED FROGS ARE DANGEROUS.
THOSE CUBAN TREE FROGS CAN'T KILL YOU, BUT THEY DO HAVE A POISON THAT COULD REALLY STING YOUR EYES.
THEY DON'T HAVE CAMOUFLAGE LIKE OTHER ANIMALS, SO OFTEN A BRIGHTLY COLORED FROG HAS ITS DEFENSE IN ITS SKIN.
RED AND BLUE POISON DART FROGS IN CENTRAL AND SOUTH AMERICA ARE EVEN WORSE!
THEY LOOKED SO HARMLESS!
GEEZ, THANKS FOR THE SAVE, MERISSA! I'M LEARNING NOT TO MAKE JUDGMENTS ABOUT ANYTHING... OR ANYONE!

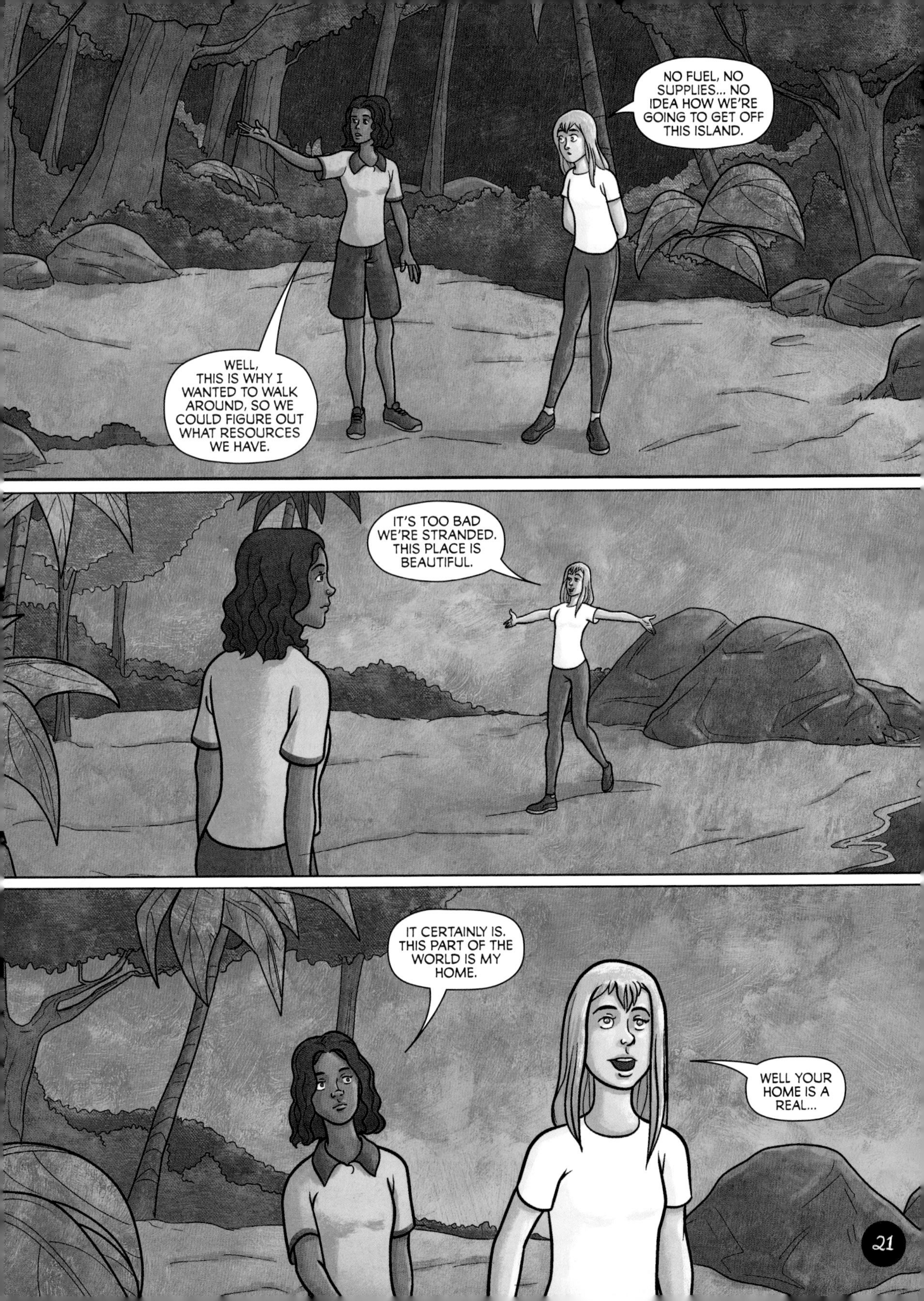
NO FUEL, NO SUPPLIES... NO IDEA HOW WE'RE GOING TO GET OFF THIS ISLAND.
WELL, THIS IS WHY I WANTED TO WALK AROUND, SO WE COULD FIGURE OUT WHAT RESOURCES WE HAVE.
IT'S TOO BAD WE'RE STRANDED. THIS PLACE IS BEAUTIFUL.
IT CERTAINLY IS. THIS PART OF THE WORLD IS MY HOME.
WELL YOUR HOME IS A REAL...

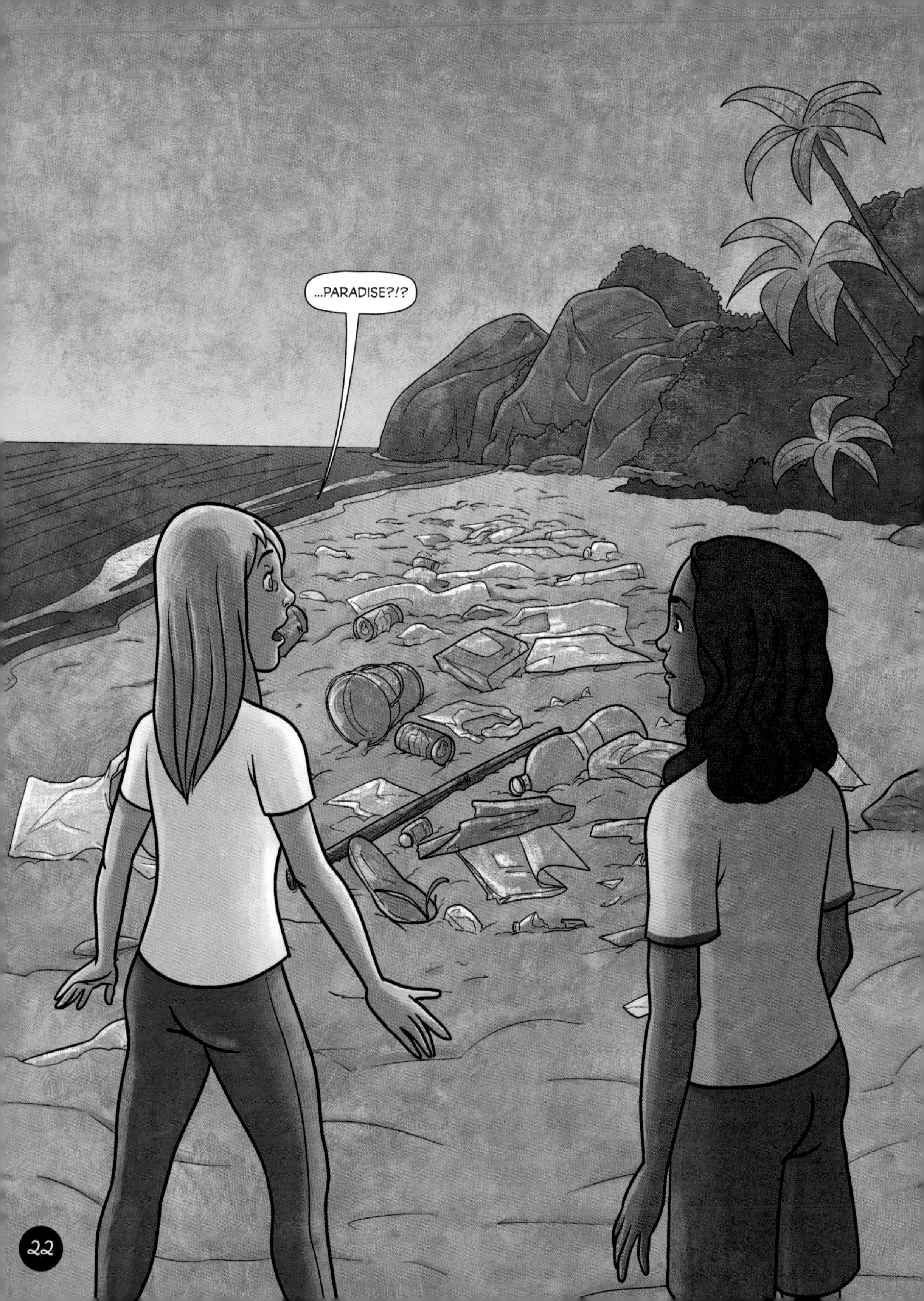
...PARADISE?!?

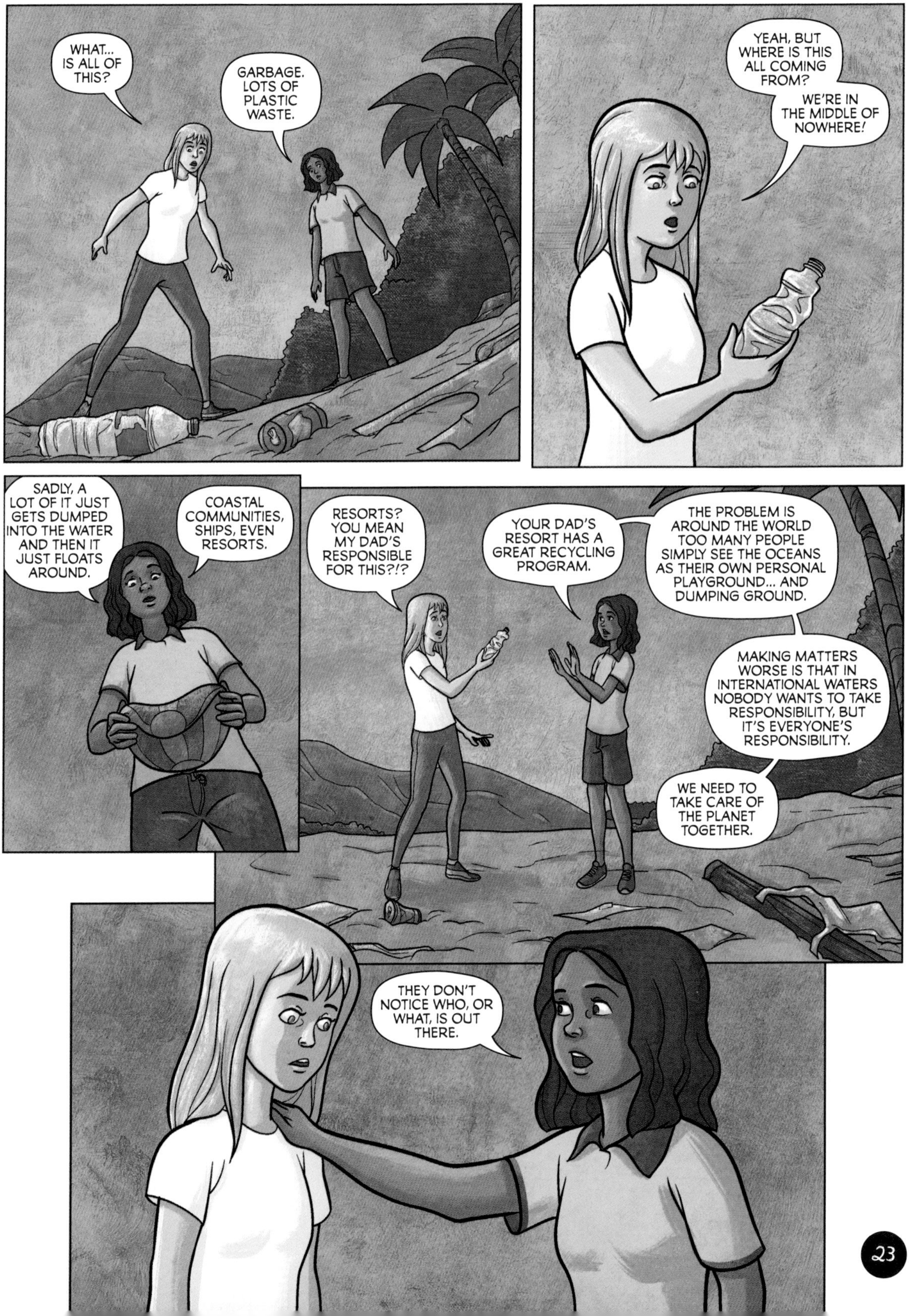
WHAT... IS ALL OF THIS?
GARBAGE. LOTS OF PLASTIC WASTE.
YEAH, BUT WHERE IS THIS ALL COMING FROM?
WE'RE IN THE MIDDLE OF NOWHERE!
SADLY, A LOT OF IT JUST GETS DUMPED INTO THE WATER AND THEN IT JUST FLOATS AROUND.
COASTAL COMMUNITIES, SHIPS, EVEN RESORTS.
RESORTS? YOU MEAN MY DAD'S RESPONSIBLE FOR THIS?!?
YOUR DAD'S RESORT HAS A GREAT RECYCLING PROGRAM.
THE PROBLEM IS AROUND THE WORLD TOO MANY PEOPLE SIMPLY SEE THE OCEANS AS THEIR OWN PERSONAL PLAYGROUND... AND DUMPING GROUND.
MAKING MATTERS WORSE IS THAT IN INTERNATIONAL WATERS NOBODY WANTS TO TAKE RESPONSIBILITY, BUT IT'S EVERYONE'S RESPONSIBILITY.
WE NEED TO TAKE CARE OF THE PLANET TOGETHER.
THEY DON'T NOTICE WHO, OR WHAT, IS OUT THERE.

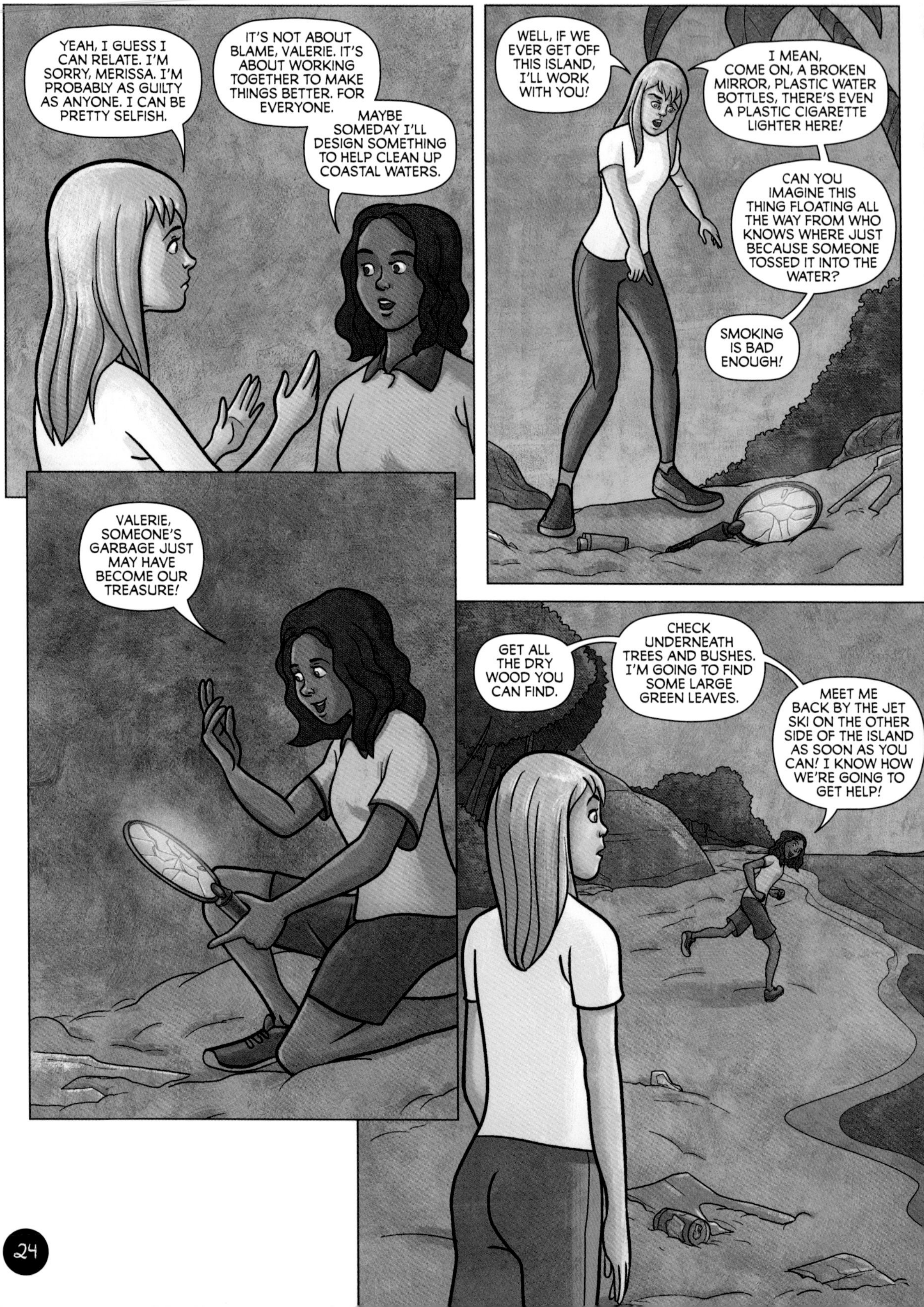
YEAH, I GUESS I CAN RELATE. I'M SORRY, MERISSA. I'M PROBABLY AS GUILTY AS ANYONE. I CAN BE PRETTY SELFISH.
IT'S NOT ABOUT BLAME, VALERIE. IT'S ABOUT WORKING TOGETHER TO MAKE THINGS BETTER. FOR EVERYONE.
MAYBE SOMEDAY I'LL DESIGN SOMETHING TO HELP CLEAN UP COASTAL WATERS.
WELL, IF WE EVER GET OFF THIS ISLAND, I'LL WORK WITH YOU!
I MEAN, COME ON, A BROKEN MIRROR, PLASTIC WATER BOTTLES, THERE'S EVEN A PLASTIC CIGARETTE LIGHTER HERE!
CAN YOU IMAGINE THIS THING FLOATING ALL THE WAY FROM WHO KNOWS WHERE JUST BECAUSE SOMEONE TOSSED IT INTO THE WATER?
SMOKING IS BAD ENOUGH!
VALERIE, SOMEONE'S GARBAGE JUST MAY HAVE BECOME OUR TREASURE!
GET ALL THE DRY WOOD YOU CAN FIND.
CHECK UNDERNEATH TREES AND BUSHES. I'M GOING TO FIND SOME LARGE GREEN LEAVES.
MEET ME BACK BY THE JET SKI ON THE OTHER SIDE OF THE ISLAND AS SOON AS YOU CAN! I KNOW HOW WE'RE GOING TO GET HELP!

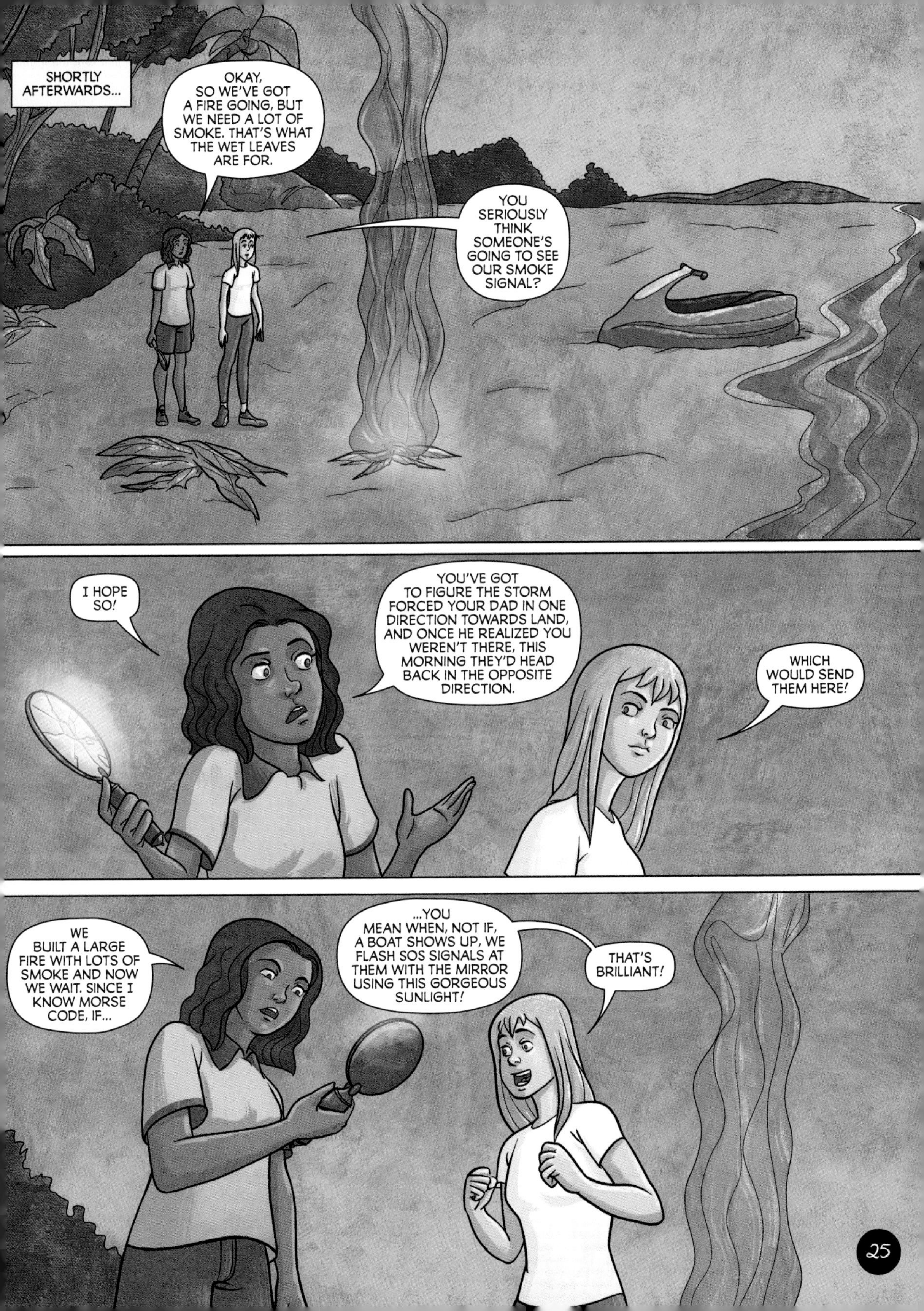
SHORTLY AFTERWARDS...
OKAY, SO WE'VE GOT A FIRE GOING, BUT WE NEED A LOT OF SMOKE. THAT'S WHAT THE WET LEAVES ARE FOR.
YOU SERIOUSLY THINK SOMEONE'S GOING TO SEE OUR SMOKE SIGNAL?
I HOPE SO!
YOU'VE GOT TO FIGURE THE STORM FORCED YOUR DAD IN ONE DIRECTION TOWARDS LAND, AND ONCE HE REALIZED YOU WEREN'T THERE, THIS MORNING THEY'D HEAD BACK IN THE OPPOSITE DIRECTION.
WHICH WOULD SEND THEM HERE!
WE BUILT A LARGE FIRE WITH LOTS OF SMOKE AND NOW WE WAIT. SINCE I KNOW MORSE CODE, IF...
...YOU MEAN WHEN, NOT IF, A BOAT SHOWS UP, WE FLASH SOS SIGNALS AT THEM WITH THE MIRROR USING THIS GORGEOUS SUNLIGHT!
THAT'S BRILLIANT!

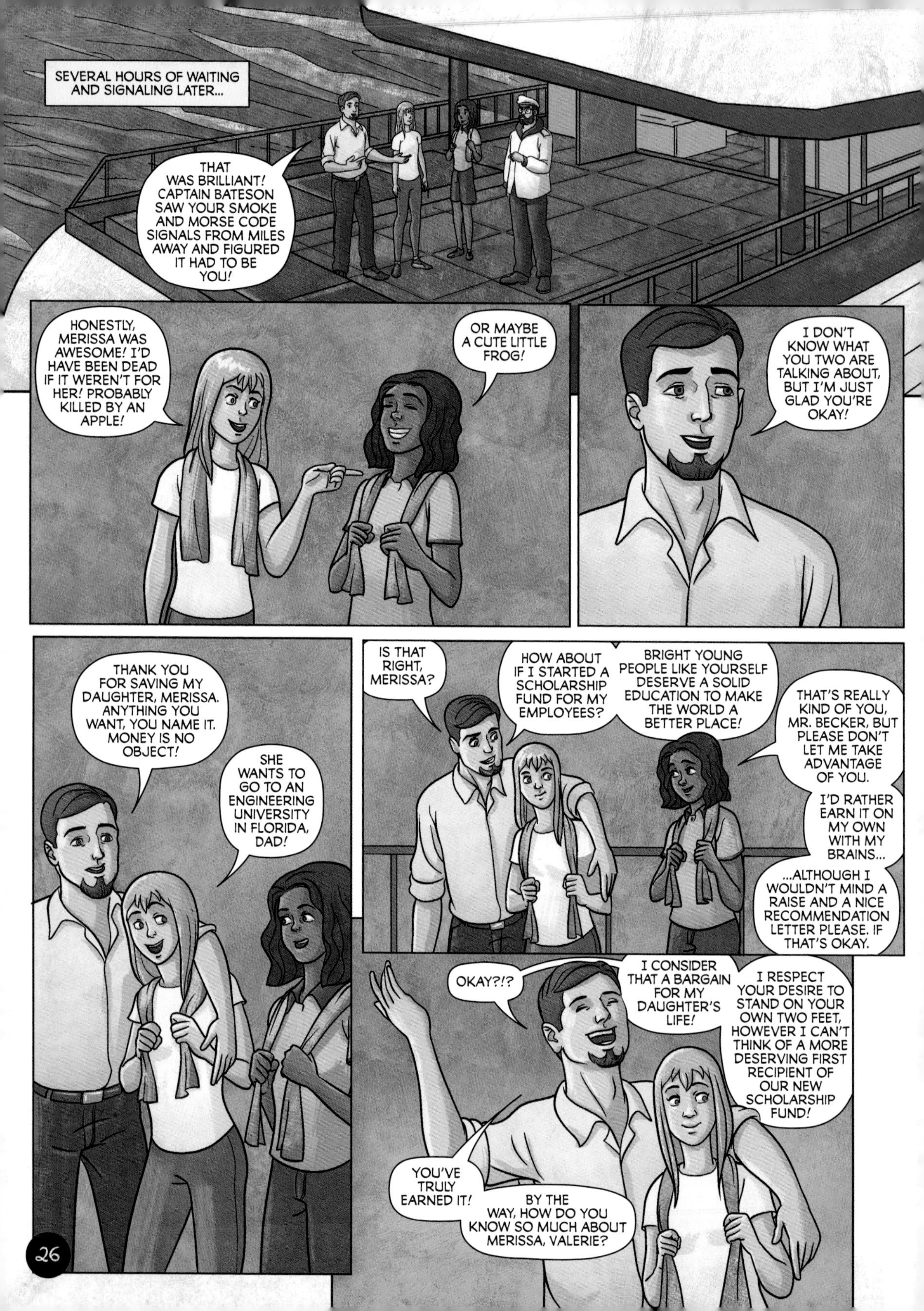
SEVERAL HOURS OF WAITING AND SIGNALING LATER...
THAT WAS BRILLIANT! CAPTAIN BATESON SAW YOUR SMOKE AND MORSE CODE SIGNALS FROM MILES AWAY AND FIGURED IT HAD TO BE YOU!
HONESTLY, MERISSA WAS AWESOME! I'D HAVE BEEN DEAD IF IT WEREN'T FOR HER! PROBABLY KILLED BY AN APPLE!
OR MAYBE A CUTE LITTLE FROG!
I DON'T KNOW WHAT YOU TWO ARE TALKING ABOUT, BUT I'M JUST GLAD YOU'RE OKAY!
THANK YOU FOR SAVING MY DAUGHTER, MERISSA. ANYTHING YOU WANT, YOU NAME IT. MONEY IS NO OBJECT!
SHE WANTS TO GO TO AN ENGINEERING UNIVERSITY IN FLORIDA, DAD!
IS THAT RIGHT, MERISSA?
HOW ABOUT IF I STARTED A SCHOLARSHIP FUND FOR MY EMPLOYEES?
BRIGHT YOUNG PEOPLE LIKE YOURSELF DESERVE A SOLID EDUCATION TO MAKE THE WORLD A BETTER PLACE!
THAT'S REALLY KIND OF YOU, MR. BECKER, BUT PLEASE DON'T LET ME TAKE ADVANTAGE OF YOU.
I'D RATHER EARN IT ON MY OWN WITH MY BRAINS...
...ALTHOUGH I WOULDN'T MIND A RAISE AND A NICE RECOMMENDATION LETTER PLEASE. IF THAT'S OKAY.
OKAY?!?
I CONSIDER THAT A BARGAIN FOR MY DAUGHTER'S LIFE!
I RESPECT YOUR DESIRE TO STAND ON YOUR OWN TWO FEET, HOWEVER I CAN'T THINK OF A MORE DESERVING FIRST RECIPIENT OF OUR NEW SCHOLARSHIP FUND!
YOU'VE TRULY EARNED IT!
BY THE WAY, HOW DO YOU KNOW SO MUCH ABOUT MERISSA, VALERIE?

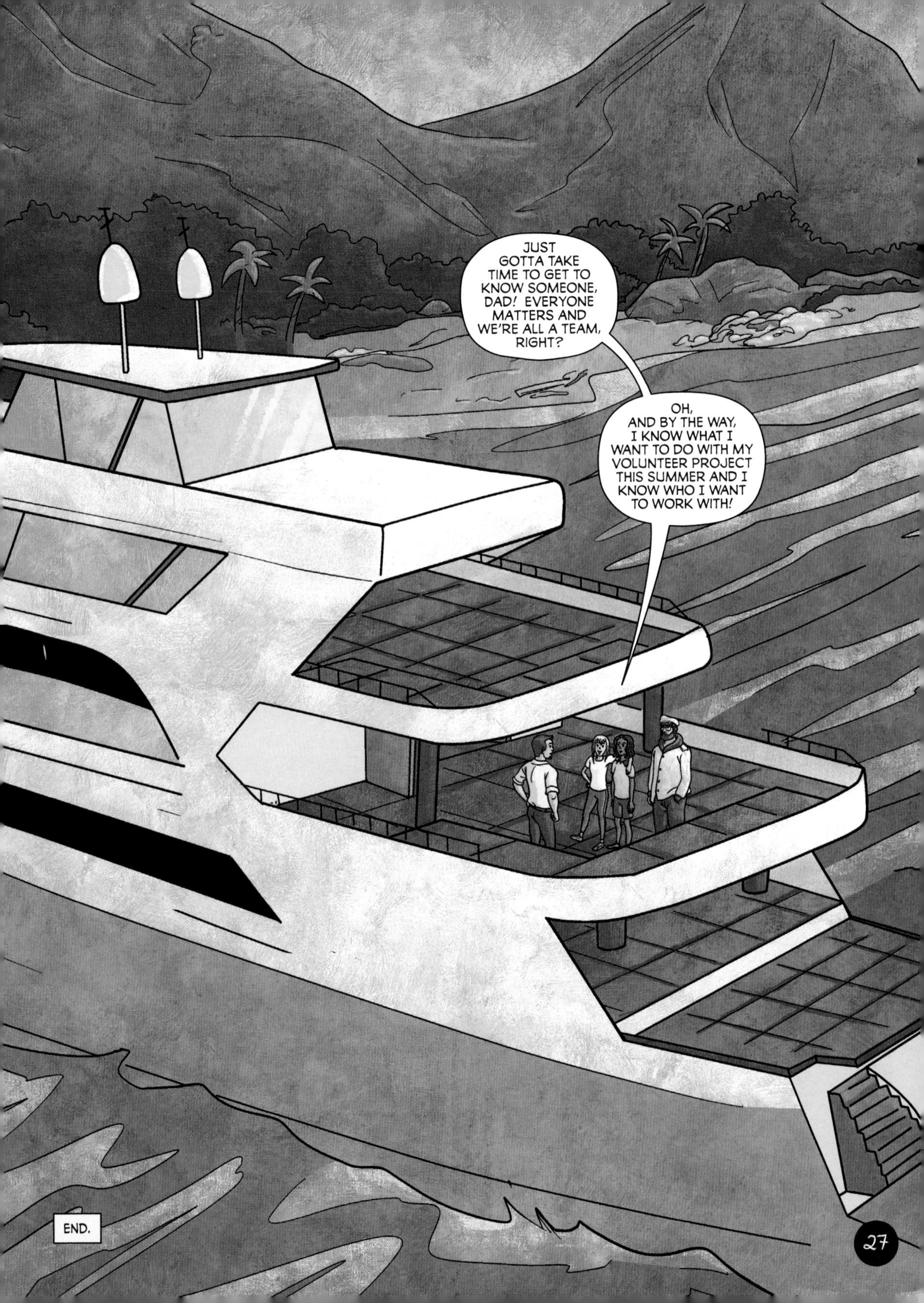
JUST GOTTA TAKE TIME TO GET TO KNOW SOMEONE, DAD! EVERYONE MATTERS AND WE'RE ALL A TEAM, RIGHT?
OH, AND BY THE WAY, I KNOW WHAT I WANT TO DO WITH MY VOLUNTEER PROJECT THIS SUMMER AND I KNOW WHO I WANT TO WORK WITH!
END.

Island Survival Guide

The Rule of Three

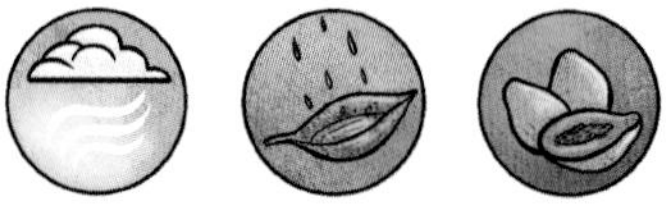

People need air, food, water, and shelter in order to survive. When you're in desperate situations, remember the Rule of Three. Usually, the longest a person should go and still have body function is three minutes without air, three hours without shelter in an extreme environment, three days without water, and three weeks without food. There can be incredible survival stories that differ from these guidelines, but the Rule of Three is a good rule of thumb.

Hello Hydration

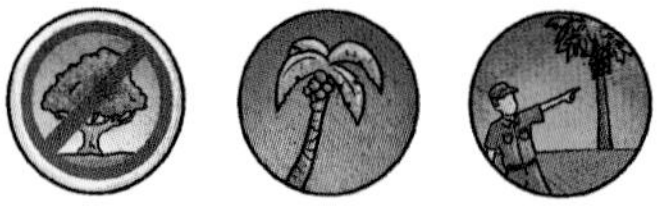

Clean drinking water is critical to human survival. It keeps your blood flowing well, your digestive system working properly, and helps keep your brain focused and alert. The average person needs about half a gallon (2 l) of water a day depending on activity level. When out in nature, try not to drink still or slow-moving water from ponds, lakes, or rivers. Bacteria can easily form in these sources. Small, flowing streams are better as less bacteria forms in these. Drinking salt water from the ocean is never a good idea unless it can be distilled and purified as it can cause severe dehydration. Collecting rainwater is safest. Collecting moisture using condensation is safe, but not as quick or easy. To be safe, always try to filter and boil the water to remove debris and kill bacteria. Boil the filtered water for at least 10 minutes and then cool it down until it is safe to drink.

Looks Can Be Deceiving...

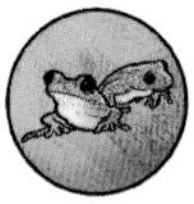
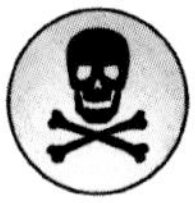
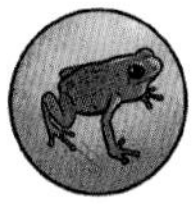

Animals that are generally seen as nonthreatening are not always safe. Look at frogs; they seem harmless and don't have claws or fangs. However, for protection, nature has equipped many species of frogs with glands that secrete poison through their skin. Sometimes the secretions can make the frogs taste terrible to predators. They can also be deadly. In most cases, brightly colored frogs look beautiful, but are poisonous. Their ability to sit out in the open with predators all around comes with either extreme confidence or extreme survival adaptations! Look, but definitely don't touch!

Splish Splash,
This Skill Could Save Your Life!

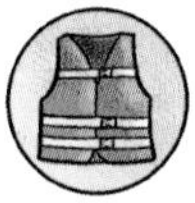
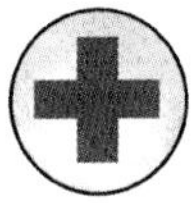
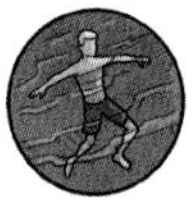

Swimming is great exercise and also opens you up to new sports. And if you live near open water, knowing how to swim is essential to survival. However, no matter where you live, it's a life skill that can come in handy for anyone. Life jackets are essential when traveling on water, but what if you don't have one in an emergency? At the very least you should learn how to tread water until help can arrive in case of a water-related emergency. There are many ways to tread water. One of the easiest is to move your arms horizontally in front of you, hands closed, with palms cupping water in the direction your hands are moving. At the same time, move your legs in a circular "bicycle pedal" motion. Contact the Red Cross or a local community pool for more information on lessons as you never know when this could come in handy!

What Do You Think?

People should be treated with respect no matter their differences. Often, it's those differences that allow people to learn and grow!

- One of the themes in this story is that looks can be deceiving. What were three examples of this in the story? It can be about plants, animals, people, or the environment. Describe what you or the characters learned.

- Describe a time when you made assumptions about someone based on that person being different from you. What did you discover about him or her? What did that teach you?

- Why do you think it was so important to Mr. Becker to treat all of his employees with respect? What was he trying to teach Valerie?

- What was the environmental issue that Valerie discovered? How does this problem relate to the theme of respect? What are some solutions you can think of to help?

- What do you think Valerie decided upon as her summer volunteer project? What are some things you'd volunteer to do to help at home or around the world?

Island Survival Trivia

1. The idea of being stranded on a desert island is not new. Books, TV shows, and movies like *Swiss Family Robinson, Survivor, Cast Away, Lord of the Flies, Robinson Crusoe,* and *Lost* have made fans all around the world wonder how they would survive!

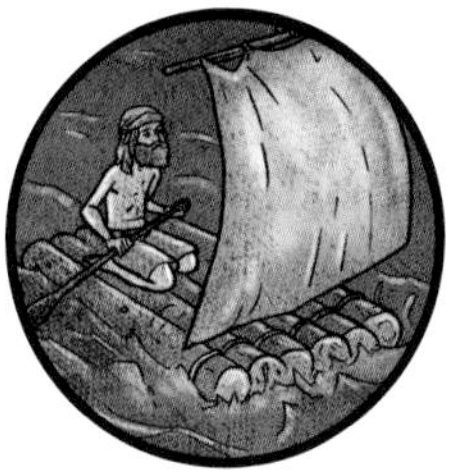

2. Often stories with people stranded on deserted islands have the characters using coconuts to survive. Did you know that the coconut can be considered a fruit, a nut, or a seed depending on what part of the plant you're investigating?

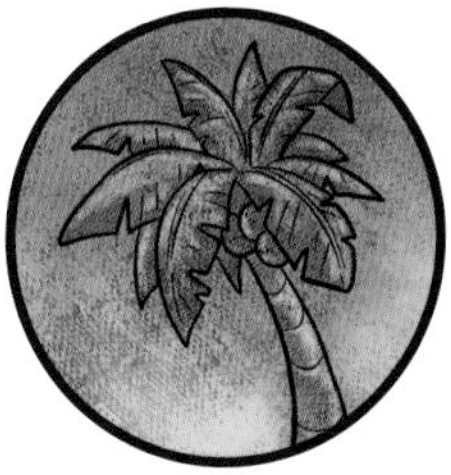

3. Many people believe that SOS means "save our ship" or "save our souls." However, it isn't an acronym at all. It's a specific distress signal!

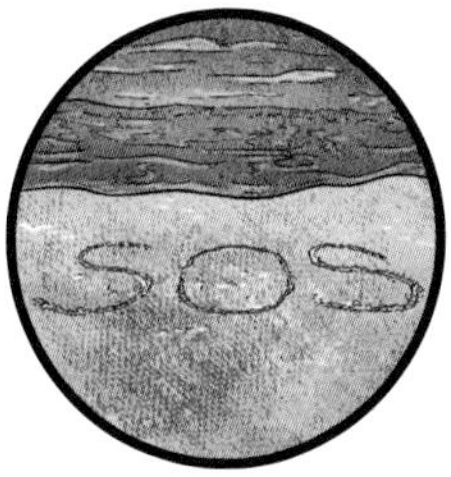
SOS

4. There are reportedly more than five TRILLION pieces of plastic that together weigh more than 250,000 tons (226,800 t) floating in the world's waters. Some have created islands of plastic. We all need to do our part to keep our planet and its waters clean!

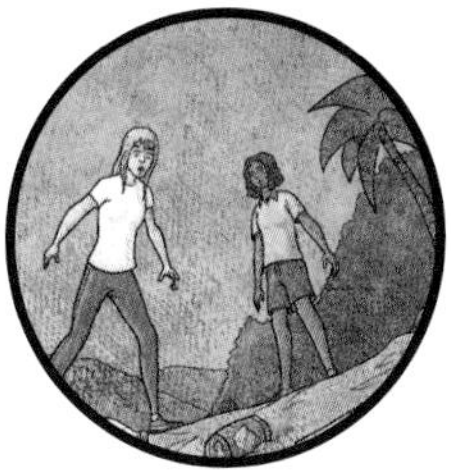

5. Christopher Columbus is often celebrated for discovering America. But did you know he was actually lost and had ended up in the Caribbean while looking for India? He never set foot on the land that we know as the United States of America!

Glossary

- **acknowledge** – to pay attention to and to greet respectfully.

- **dehydration** – the loss or removal of water. When lost or used water is not replaced, a person becomes dehydrated.

- **forecasts** – weather predictions.

- **helm** – the steering and control area of a ship.

- **moor** – tie down securely.

- **Morse code** – an international communication method using dots and dashes, or long and short tones or signals.

- **nautical** – to do with ships and sailing.

Online Resources

Booklinks
NONFICTION NETWORK
FREE! ONLINE NONFICTION RESOURCES

To learn more about ocean survival, please visit **abdobooklinks.com** or scan this QR code. These links are routinely monitored and updated to provide the most current information available.